The Haunted Castle

Fantasy fiction, Volume 7

Sarah Elizabeth Davis

Published by Arcane Horizons Publishing, 2024.

This is a work of fiction. Similarities to real people, places, or events are entirely coincidental.

THE HAUNTED CASTLE

First edition. August 5, 2024.

Copyright © 2024 Sarah Elizabeth Davis.

ISBN: 979-8227231017

Written by Sarah Elizabeth Davis.

Table of Contents

To those who seek the truth in the shadows and find light in the
darkest of places.

To the spirits of the past, whose stories guide our present and shape
our future.

And to the brave souls who dare to uncover the secrets that others fear
to face.

This book is for you.

Chapter 1: The Invitation

Aria sat by the window of her small apartment, staring out at the bustling city below. The sky was a dull gray, reflecting her mood. Life had been monotonous lately—work, home, and the occasional night out with friends. She craved something more, something exciting and different. Little did she know that her wish was about to be granted in the most unexpected way.

It was a chilly afternoon in late October when the letter arrived. Aria found it wedged between the usual stack of bills and advertisements. The envelope was made of thick, creamy paper, and her name was written in elegant cursive. There was no return address, only a wax seal stamped with an intricate crest she didn't recognize. Intrigued, she carefully broke the seal and unfolded the letter inside.

The letter read:

Dear Aria,

It is with great pleasure that I inform you of an unexpected inheritance. As the last living relative of the late Lord William Blackwood, you have been bequeathed the Blackwood Castle, an estate that has been in our family for centuries.

You are invited to visit the castle at your earliest convenience to meet with the caretaker, Mr. Blackwood, and learn more about your inheritance.

Yours sincerely,

Margaret Ashford

Estate Solicitor

ARIA READ THE LETTER twice, unable to believe her eyes. Inheritance? A castle? It sounded like something out of a fairy tale. She had no knowledge of any distant relatives, let alone a castle-owning lord. Curiosity sparked, she decided to call the number listed at the bottom of the letter.

Margaret Ashford answered after a few rings, her voice warm and professional. "Margaret Ashford speaking. How may I assist you?"

"Hello, this is Aria. I received a letter regarding an inheritance. I wanted to confirm if this is real. It sounds too good to be true."

"I assure you, Miss Aria, it is very much real. Blackwood Castle has been in your family for generations. Lord William Blackwood was a distant relative, and as the last living heir, you are entitled to the estate."

"Why didn't I know about this before?" Aria asked, still trying to wrap her head around the situation.

"Lord William was a reclusive man, and his passing was a rather private affair. His solicitor, myself, was instructed to find the rightful heir, which turned out to be you. If you wish to see the castle and discuss further details, I can arrange for your visit."

Aria hesitated for a moment. The logical part of her brain urged caution, but the adventurous side won over. "I'd like to visit the castle," she said, feeling a surge of excitement.

"Excellent. I'll arrange for Mr. Blackwood, the caretaker, to meet you there. When would be convenient for you?"

"Is this weekend too soon?"

"Not at all. I'll notify Mr. Blackwood of your arrival. The castle is located in the countryside, a few hours' drive from the city. I'll email you the directions and necessary details. Safe travels, Miss Aria."

After hanging up, Aria couldn't contain her excitement. She called her best friend, Lily, to share the news.

"A castle? Are you serious?" Lily exclaimed. "That's incredible! You have to take me with you."

"Of course, I wouldn't want to go alone," Aria replied. "It'll be an adventure."

The following days flew by in a blur of preparation. Aria packed her bags, ensuring she had everything she might need for a weekend at a castle. She and Lily set off early Saturday morning, eager to see the mysterious estate.

The drive was picturesque, taking them through rolling hills and quaint villages. As they left the city behind, the scenery grew more remote and wild. The GPS led them down a narrow, winding road that seemed to disappear into dense forest. After what felt like hours, they emerged into a clearing, and there it was—Blackwood Castle.

The castle stood majestically on a hill, surrounded by ancient trees. It was a sprawling structure of gray stone, with turrets and battlements that spoke of a bygone era. Ivy clung to the walls, and the windows glinted in the afternoon sun. Aria felt a shiver of awe and anticipation.

"This is amazing," Lily whispered, equally entranced by the sight.

They parked the car and made their way to the massive wooden doors. Before they could knock, the doors creaked open, and a tall, stern-looking man stepped out. He was dressed in a dark suit, his hair silver and neatly combed.

"Miss Aria, I presume?" he said, his voice deep and formal.

"Yes, and this is my friend, Lily," Aria replied.

"Welcome to Blackwood Castle. I am Mr. Blackwood, the caretaker. Please, come inside."

The interior of the castle was just as impressive as the exterior. The entrance hall was vast, with high ceilings and grand chandeliers. Portraits of stern-looking ancestors lined the walls, their eyes seeming to follow the visitors as they walked by. A grand staircase led to the upper floors, and the polished wooden floors echoed with their footsteps.

Mr. Blackwood led them to a sitting room, where a fire crackled in the hearth. "Please, make yourselves comfortable. I'll fetch some refreshments."

As they settled into the plush armchairs, Lily turned to Aria with wide eyes. "This place is incredible. I can't believe you own it."

"Neither can I," Aria admitted. "It feels like a dream."

Mr. Blackwood returned with a tray of tea and biscuits. "I'm sure you have many questions, Miss Aria. Allow me to provide some answers. Blackwood Castle has been in your family for over three hundred years. It was built by Lord William's ancestor, Sir Thomas Blackwood, in the late 17th century."

"What happened to Lord William?" Aria asked.

"Lord William passed away peacefully in his sleep six months ago. He had no immediate family, and you were the closest living relative we could find. His will stipulated that the castle be passed down to you."

"Why didn't I know about this side of the family?" Aria wondered aloud.

"Your branch of the family moved to the city several generations ago, and over time, contact was lost. Lord William himself was quite reclusive, preferring the solitude of the castle."

Aria nodded, trying to absorb the information. "What's the castle's condition? Is it livable?"

"It is, though some areas require maintenance. The castle has been preserved well, but it is an old building. I've been managing the estate for many years, and I can assure you it is safe and comfortable."

"Thank you, Mr. Blackwood. This is all so overwhelming, but I'm excited to learn more about the castle and my family's history."

"You're welcome, Miss Aria. I will give you a tour of the castle, and we can discuss any renovations or changes you wish to make."

The tour was a journey through time. Mr. Blackwood showed them the grand ballroom, the opulent dining hall, the extensive library, and the numerous bedrooms, each with its own unique character. Aria felt a deep connection to the place, as if she were rediscovering a part of herself.

They ended the tour in the garden, where the sun was setting, casting a golden glow over the landscape. "This is beautiful," Aria said, taking in the view.

"It is," Mr. Blackwood agreed. "The gardens have been meticulously maintained over the years. They are a place of peace and reflection."

Aria took a deep breath, feeling a sense of belonging she hadn't felt in a long time. "I think I'm going to like it here."

As they walked back to the castle, Aria felt a growing sense of excitement. She had inherited more than just a castle; she had inherited a piece of history, a legacy. Little did she know that this legacy came with secrets and mysteries that would soon unfold.

That night, after a hearty dinner prepared by Mr. Blackwood, Aria and Lily retired to their respective rooms. The castle was quiet, the only sounds being the crackling of the fire and the occasional creak of the old building settling. As Aria lay in bed, she couldn't help but think about the strange occurrences she had read about in the letter. Whispers and footsteps in the hallways? A ghostly figure?

She shook her head, dismissing it as her imagination running wild. Yet, as she drifted off to sleep, she couldn't shake the feeling that she was being watched.

Aria awoke with a start in the middle of the night. The room was pitch dark, the only light coming from the faint glow of the moon through the curtains. She listened intently, trying to discern what had woken her. There it was again—a soft, almost imperceptible whisper, like a breeze passing through the room.

Heart pounding, she sat up and looked around. The room appeared empty, but the whispering continued, growing louder and more distinct. It seemed to be coming from the hallway outside her door. Summoning her courage, Aria slipped out of bed and tiptoed to the door, her heart hammering in her chest.

She opened the door a crack and peered into the dimly lit hallway. To her shock, she saw a figure standing at the end of the corridor. It was a man, dressed in old-fashioned clothing, his face obscured by shadows. The whispering stopped, and the figure turned to look directly at her.

Aria's breath caught in her throat. The figure's eyes were hollow and filled with sorrow, and his expression was one of desperation. He raised a hand as if to beckon her, and then, just as suddenly as he had appeared, he vanished into thin air.

Aria slammed the door shut and leaned against it, her mind racing. Had she just seen a ghost? The logical part of her brain insisted it was a dream, a figment of her imagination. But deep down, she knew it was real.

She spent the rest of the night tossing and turning, unable to shake the image of the ghostly figure. By morning, she was exhausted but determined to find out more about the castle's haunting.

Over breakfast, she shared her experience with Lily and Mr. Blackwood. Lily looked skeptical, but Mr. Blackwood's expression was unreadable.

"I see you have encountered one of the castle's spirits," Mr. Blackwood said calmly. "That must have been Lord William. He appears occasionally, seeking something."

"Seeking what?" Aria asked, her curiosity piqued.

"No one knows for sure," Mr. Blackwood replied. "Some say he is searching for justice, others believe he is protecting the castle from some unknown threat."

"Is there any way to communicate with him?" Aria asked, feeling a strange connection to the ghost.

"There are ways, but they are risky," Mr. Blackwood cautioned. "It is best to proceed with caution and respect the spirits."

Aria nodded, determined to uncover the truth. She spent the next few days exploring the castle, reading through the old journals and books in the library, and speaking with Mr. Blackwood about the history of the estate. She learned about the various owners, the tragedies that had befallen them, and the rumors of the castle being haunted.

One afternoon, while sifting through a stack of old letters in the library, Aria came across a letter addressed to Lord William. The handwriting was shaky, and the ink had faded, but she could make out the words.

Dear William,

I fear for my life. Your brother has grown increasingly unstable and violent. I believe he plans to harm me. Please, if you receive this letter, come to my aid.

Yours in desperation,

Eleanor

ARIA'S HEART RACED as she read the letter. This was a clue, a piece of the puzzle that could explain the ghost's sorrow and desperation. She needed to find out more about Eleanor and her relationship with Lord William's brother.

She brought the letter to Mr. Blackwood, who examined it carefully. "This is significant," he said. "Eleanor was Lord William's wife, and his brother, Edward, was known for his jealousy and ambition. This letter suggests that Edward may have been responsible for William's death."

"We need to find more evidence," Aria said, determined to uncover the truth.

Mr. Blackwood nodded. "There is an old journal belonging to Eleanor. It might contain more information. I will help you find it."

They spent hours searching the library, and finally, they found the journal hidden behind a stack of old books. The leather cover was worn and cracked, and the pages were yellowed with age. Aria carefully opened it and began to read.

The journal detailed Eleanor's life at the castle, her love for William, and her growing fear of Edward. She described how Edward had become obsessed with the idea of inheriting the castle and had made several attempts to harm William. The entries became more frantic and desperate, culminating in a final, chilling entry.

William is dead. Edward has killed him, and now he comes for me. I fear I will not survive the night. If anyone finds this journal, please know that William's death was not an accident. Edward must be brought to justice.

ARIA'S HANDS TREMBLED as she read the final entry. This was the proof she needed. Lord William and Eleanor had been murdered by Edward, and their spirits were trapped in the castle, seeking justice.

"We have to do something," Aria said, her voice shaking. "We have to help them."

Mr. Blackwood nodded. "We can hold a séance to communicate with the spirits. It is risky, but it may be the only way to set them free."

Aria agreed, and they began to prepare for the séance. They gathered candles, incense, and a crystal ball, and set up a circle in the library. As night fell, they lit the candles and sat in the circle, holding hands.

Mr. Blackwood began to chant, calling upon the spirits to join them. The air grew cold, and the flames flickered. Aria felt a chill run down her spine as the room filled with an eerie presence.

Suddenly, the crystal ball began to glow, and a misty figure appeared. It was Lord William, his eyes filled with sorrow.

"Who are you?" Mr. Blackwood asked.

"I am William Blackwood," the ghost replied, his voice echoing through the room. "I seek justice for my wife and myself. We were betrayed by my brother, Edward."

"We have proof," Aria said, holding up the journal. "Eleanor wrote about what happened. We can help you."

The ghost looked at the journal, his expression softening. "Thank you. You are brave to help us. But be warned, Edward's spirit is still here, and he will not let us go easily."

The room grew colder, and a dark, malevolent presence filled the air. Aria's heart pounded as she felt the anger and hatred emanating from the spirit of Edward.

"You will not escape," a voice hissed, filled with venom. "This castle is mine."

The candles flickered and went out, plunging the room into darkness. Aria felt a cold hand grasp her arm, and she screamed. The circle broke, and chaos ensued. Books flew off the shelves, and the furniture shook.

"Hold on!" Mr. Blackwood shouted, his voice barely audible over the commotion. "We must finish the séance!"

Aria struggled to stay focused, her mind racing. She reached out and grabbed the crystal ball, concentrating all her energy on the spirits of William and Eleanor.

"Leave us in peace!" she cried, her voice filled with determination. "You cannot keep them here forever!"

The room shook violently, and then, just as suddenly as it had started, the chaos stopped. The air grew still, and the dark presence dissipated. The candles relit themselves, casting a warm glow over the room.

Lord William and Eleanor appeared, their expressions filled with gratitude. "Thank you," William said. "You have freed us."

Aria felt a sense of relief wash over her. "What will happen now?"

"We will finally find peace," Eleanor said, her voice soft and serene. "The castle is yours now, to care for and protect."

With that, the spirits faded away, leaving Aria and Mr. Blackwood alone in the library. Aria felt a weight lift from her shoulders, knowing that she had done the right thing.

As dawn broke, she and Mr. Blackwood sat in the garden, reflecting on the events of the night. "You were brave," Mr. Blackwood said. "Not many would have faced the spirits so fearlessly."

Aria smiled. "I couldn't have done it without your help. Thank you."

"You have a strong spirit," Mr. Blackwood replied. "The castle is in good hands."

Aria looked out at the sunrise, feeling a sense of peace and belonging. She had inherited more than just a castle; she had inherited a legacy of courage and resilience. And she knew that, whatever challenges lay ahead, she was ready to face them.

Thus began Aria's journey at Blackwood Castle, a journey filled with mystery, adventure, and the promise of new beginnings.

Chapter 2: Arrival at the Castle

The drive to Blackwood Castle took longer than Aria had anticipated. The cityscape gradually gave way to the rolling countryside, and the roads grew narrower and less maintained as they approached their destination. As the car climbed the final hill, the castle came into view, looming against the twilight sky like a brooding sentinel of history.

Aria's heart raced with anticipation as she and Lily drove through the iron gates that creaked open, as if welcoming them into another world. The gravel driveway crunched beneath the tires, winding through ancient oaks whose branches seemed to reach out in silent greeting. They parked in front of the castle's grand entrance, and for a moment, Aria simply sat, taking it all in.

The castle was everything she had imagined and more. Its gray stone walls, covered in ivy, seemed to exude a life of their own. Tall, narrow windows stared out like watchful eyes, and the twin turrets rose high into the sky, their tips lost in the gathering dusk. It was both magnificent and intimidating, a relic of a bygone era standing steadfast against the march of time.

"This place is incredible," Lily murmured, breaking the silence. "It's like something out of a gothic novel."

Aria nodded, her thoughts echoing Lily's sentiments. She took a deep breath, steeling herself for what lay ahead. "Let's go meet Mr. Blackwood," she said, stepping out of the car.

As they approached the massive wooden doors, they opened with a slow, deliberate creak, revealing a tall, stern-looking man dressed in a dark suit. His silver hair was neatly combed, and his piercing blue eyes seemed to see right through them.

"Miss Aria, welcome to Blackwood Castle," he said, his voice deep and formal. "I am Mr. Blackwood, the caretaker. And you must be Miss Lily."

Lily nodded, offering a polite smile. "Yes, thank you for having us."

"Please, come inside," Mr. Blackwood said, stepping aside to allow them entry.

The entrance hall was vast, with high ceilings and grand chandeliers that cast a warm, golden light. The air was filled with the scent of aged wood and a hint of something floral. Aria's footsteps echoed on the polished stone floor as she took in the opulence around her. Portraits of stern-looking ancestors lined the walls, their eyes seeming to follow her every move.

Mr. Blackwood led them to a sitting room, where a fire crackled in the hearth, casting flickering shadows on the walls. "Please, make yourselves comfortable," he said. "I will fetch some refreshments."

Aria and Lily sank into the plush armchairs, grateful for the warmth of the fire. They exchanged glances, both of them feeling the weight of the castle's history pressing down on them.

"This place is amazing," Lily whispered. "But there's something...off about it."

Aria nodded. "I know what you mean. It's like the walls are hiding secrets."

Mr. Blackwood returned with a tray of tea and biscuits. "I'm sure you have many questions, Miss Aria. Allow me to provide some answers."

Aria took a cup of tea, savoring the warmth. "Thank you, Mr. Blackwood. I'm curious about the castle's history. How long has it been in my family?"

"Blackwood Castle has been in your family for over three hundred years," Mr. Blackwood replied. "It was built by Sir Thomas Blackwood in the late 17th century. Each generation has added to the estate, making it what it is today."

"What happened to Lord William?" Aria asked, her curiosity piqued.

"Lord William passed away peacefully in his sleep six months ago. He had no immediate family, and you were the closest living relative we could find. His will stipulated that the castle be passed down to you."

Aria nodded, still trying to wrap her head around the idea of inheriting a castle. "Why didn't I know about this side of the family?"

"Your branch of the family moved to the city several generations ago, and over time, contact was lost. Lord William himself was quite reclusive, preferring the solitude of the castle."

"Is the castle livable?" Lily asked, looking around.

"It is, though some areas require maintenance," Mr. Blackwood replied. "The castle has been preserved well, but it is an old building. I have been managing the estate for many years, and I can assure you it is safe and comfortable."

"Thank you, Mr. Blackwood," Aria said. "This is all so overwhelming, but I'm excited to learn more about the castle and my family's history."

"You're welcome, Miss Aria. I will give you a tour of the castle, and we can discuss any renovations or changes you wish to make."

The tour began in the entrance hall, where Mr. Blackwood pointed out the intricate carvings on the wooden staircase and the stained glass windows that depicted scenes from the castle's history. Aria couldn't help but feel a sense of awe as she imagined the generations of her family who had walked these halls.

They moved on to the grand ballroom, a vast space with a high, vaulted ceiling and crystal chandeliers that sparkled in the light. "This room has hosted many grand events over the centuries," Mr. Blackwood said. "Balls, banquets, and even a few royal visits."

Aria could almost hear the echo of music and laughter, see the elegantly dressed guests dancing under the chandeliers. It was like stepping back in time.

Next, they visited the dining hall, with its long, polished table and high-backed chairs. The walls were lined with tapestries depicting scenes of hunting and feasting. "This is where the family would gather for meals," Mr. Blackwood explained. "It has not been used in some time, but it is still in excellent condition."

The library was Aria's favorite room. Shelves lined the walls, filled with leather-bound books that smelled of old paper and ink. A large, ornate desk stood in the center of the room, and a cozy reading nook with a window seat overlooked the gardens. "The library contains many rare and valuable volumes," Mr. Blackwood said. "Some date back to the time of Sir Thomas Blackwood."

Aria ran her fingers over the spines of the books, feeling a sense of connection to her ancestors. "I could spend days in here," she said, her eyes shining with excitement.

"There is much to discover," Mr. Blackwood agreed. "Many of the books contain personal journals and letters that detail the history of the family and the castle."

They continued the tour, visiting the numerous bedrooms, each with its own unique character. Some were grand and opulent, others more modest and cozy. Aria's room was one of the former, with a four-poster bed, rich tapestries, and a view of the gardens.

The tour ended in the garden, where the sun was setting, casting a golden glow over the landscape. The garden was a maze of hedges, flower beds, and ancient trees, with a fountain in the center that sparkled in the fading light. "The gardens have been meticulously maintained over the years," Mr. Blackwood said. "They are a place of peace and reflection."

Aria took a deep breath, feeling a sense of belonging she hadn't felt in a long time. "I think I'm going to like it here."

As they walked back to the castle, Aria felt a growing sense of excitement. She had inherited more than just a castle; she had inherited a piece of history, a legacy. But with that legacy came questions and mysteries that she was determined to unravel.

That night, after a hearty dinner prepared by Mr. Blackwood, Aria and Lily retired to their respective rooms. The castle was quiet, the only sounds being the crackling of the fire and the occasional creak of the old building settling. As Aria lay in bed, she couldn't help but think about the strange occurrences she had read about in the letter. Whispers and footsteps in the hallways? A ghostly figure?

She shook her head, dismissing it as her imagination running wild. Yet, as she drifted off to sleep, she couldn't shake the feeling that she was being watched.

Aria awoke with a start in the middle of the night. The room was pitch dark, the only light coming from the faint glow of the moon through the curtains. She listened intently, trying to discern what had woken her. There it was again—a soft, almost imperceptible whisper, like a breeze passing through the room.

Heart pounding, she sat up and looked around. The room appeared empty, but the whispering continued, growing louder and more distinct. It seemed to be coming from the hallway outside her door. Summoning her courage, Aria slipped out of bed and tiptoed to the door, her heart hammering in her chest.

She opened the door a crack and peered into the dimly lit hallway. To her shock, she saw a figure standing at the end of the corridor. It was a man, dressed in old-fashioned clothing, his face obscured by shadows. The whispering stopped, and the figure turned to look directly at her.

Aria's breath caught in her throat. The figure's eyes were hollow and filled with sorrow, and his expression was one of desperation. He raised a hand as if to beckon her, and then, just as suddenly as he had appeared, he vanished into thin air.

Aria slammed the door shut and leaned against it, her mind racing. Had she just seen a ghost? The logical part of her brain insisted it was a dream, a figment of her imagination. But deep down, she knew it was real.

She spent the rest of the night tossing and turning, unable to shake the image of the ghostly figure. By morning, she was exhausted but determined to find out more about the castle's haunting.

Over breakfast, she shared her experience with Lily and Mr. Blackwood. Lily looked skeptical, but Mr. Blackwood's expression was unreadable.

"I see you have encountered one of the castle's spirits," Mr. Blackwood said calmly. "That must have been Lord William. He appears occasionally, seeking something."

"Seeking what?" Aria asked, her curiosity piqued.

"No one knows for sure," Mr. Blackwood replied. "Some say he is searching for justice, others believe he is protecting the castle from some unknown threat."

"Is there any way to communicate with him?" Aria asked, feeling a strange connection to the ghost.

"There are ways, but they are risky," Mr. Blackwood cautioned. "It is best to proceed with caution and respect the spirits."

Aria nodded, determined to uncover the truth. She spent the next few days exploring the castle, reading through the old journals and books in the library, and speaking with Mr. Blackwood about the history of the estate. She learned about the various owners, the tragedies that had befallen them, and the rumors of the castle being haunted.

One afternoon, while sifting through a stack of old letters in the library, Aria came across a letter addressed to Lord William. The handwriting was shaky, and the ink had faded, but she could make out the words.

Dear William,

I fear for my life. Your brother has grown increasingly unstable and violent. I believe he plans to harm me. Please, if you receive this letter, come to my aid.

Yours in desperation,

Eleanor

ARIA'S HEART RACED as she read the letter. This was a clue, a piece of the puzzle that could explain the ghost's sorrow and desperation. She needed to find out more about Eleanor and her relationship with Lord William's brother.

She brought the letter to Mr. Blackwood, who examined it carefully. "This is significant," he said. "Eleanor was Lord William's wife, and his brother, Edward, was known for his jealousy and ambition. This letter suggests that Edward may have been responsible for William's death."

"We need to find more evidence," Aria said, determined to uncover the truth.

Mr. Blackwood nodded. "There is an old journal belonging to Eleanor. It might contain more information. I will help you find it."

They spent hours searching the library, and finally, they found the journal hidden behind a stack of old books. The leather cover was worn and cracked, and the pages were yellowed with age. Aria carefully opened it and began to read.

The journal detailed Eleanor's life at the castle, her love for William, and her growing fear of Edward. She described how Edward had become obsessed with the idea of inheriting the castle and had made several attempts to harm William. The entries became more frantic and desperate, culminating in a final, chilling entry.

William is dead. Edward has killed him, and now he comes for me. I fear I will not survive the night. If anyone finds this journal, please know that William's death was not an accident. Edward must be brought to justice.

ARIA'S HANDS TREMBLED as she read the final entry. This was the proof she needed. Lord William and Eleanor had been murdered by Edward, and their spirits were trapped in the castle, seeking justice.

"We have to do something," Aria said, her voice shaking. "We have to help them."

Mr. Blackwood nodded. "We can hold a séance to communicate with the spirits. It is risky, but it may be the only way to set them free."

Aria agreed, and they began to prepare for the séance. They gathered candles, incense, and a crystal ball, and set up a circle in the library. As night fell, they lit the candles and sat in the circle, holding hands.

Mr. Blackwood began to chant, calling upon the spirits to join them. The air grew cold, and the flames flickered. Aria felt a chill run down her spine as the room filled with an eerie presence.

Suddenly, the crystal ball began to glow, and a misty figure appeared. It was Lord William, his eyes filled with sorrow.

"Who are you?" Mr. Blackwood asked.

"I am William Blackwood," the ghost replied, his voice echoing through the room. "I seek justice for my wife and myself. We were betrayed by my brother, Edward."

"We have proof," Aria said, holding up the journal. "Eleanor wrote about what happened. We can help you."

The ghost looked at the journal, his expression softening. "Thank you. You are brave to help us. But be warned, Edward's spirit is still here, and he will not let us go easily."

The room grew colder, and a dark, malevolent presence filled the air. Aria's heart pounded as she felt the anger and hatred emanating from the spirit of Edward.

"You will not escape," a voice hissed, filled with venom. "This castle is mine."

The candles flickered and went out, plunging the room into darkness. Aria felt a cold hand grasp her arm, and she screamed. The circle broke, and chaos ensued. Books flew off the shelves, and the furniture shook.

"Hold on!" Mr. Blackwood shouted, his voice barely audible over the commotion. "We must finish the séance!"

Aria struggled to stay focused, her mind racing. She reached out and grabbed the crystal ball, concentrating all her energy on the spirits of William and Eleanor.

"Leave us in peace!" she cried, her voice filled with determination. "You cannot keep them here forever!"

The room shook violently, and then, just as suddenly as it had started, the chaos stopped. The air grew still, and the dark presence dissipated. The candles relit themselves, casting a warm glow over the room.

Lord William and Eleanor appeared, their expressions filled with gratitude. "Thank you," William said. "You have freed us."

Aria felt a sense of relief wash over her. "What will happen now?"

"We will finally find peace," Eleanor said, her voice soft and serene. "The castle is yours now, to care for and protect."

With that, the spirits faded away, leaving Aria and Mr. Blackwood alone in the library. Aria felt a weight lift from her shoulders, knowing that she had done the right thing.

As dawn broke, she and Mr. Blackwood sat in the garden, reflecting on the events of the night. "You were brave," Mr. Blackwood said. "Not many would have faced the spirits so fearlessly."

Aria smiled. "I couldn't have done it without your help. Thank you."

"You have a strong spirit," Mr. Blackwood replied. "The castle is in good hands."

Aria looked out at the sunrise, feeling a sense of peace and belonging. She had inherited more than just a castle; she had inherited a legacy of courage and resilience. And she knew that, whatever challenges lay ahead, she was ready to face them.

Thus began Aria's journey at Blackwood Castle, a journey filled with mystery, adventure, and the promise of new beginnings.

Chapter 3: The First Night

The shadows lengthened across the grounds of Blackwood Castle as the sun dipped below the horizon, casting the ancient stone walls in an eerie, otherworldly glow. Aria stood at the window of her bedroom, watching the last sliver of daylight disappear, feeling a mixture of excitement and apprehension. The castle was beautiful, but it also held an undeniable aura of mystery and secrets long forgotten.

Lily had retired to her room early, exhausted from the day's journey and the emotional whirlwind of discovering Aria's inheritance. Aria, however, was too wired to sleep. She decided to spend some time in the library, exploring the volumes of history and lore that filled the shelves. She slipped on a comfortable sweater and made her way down the dimly lit corridors, her footsteps echoing softly on the stone floors.

The library was a sanctuary of knowledge and history. Shelves lined the walls, filled with leather-bound books that smelled of old paper and ink. A large, ornate desk stood in the center of the room, and a cozy reading nook with a window seat overlooked the gardens. Aria ran her fingers over the spines of the books, feeling a sense of connection to her ancestors.

She selected a book on the history of the Blackwood family and settled into the window seat. As she read, the wind howled outside, rattling the windowpanes. The castle creaked and groaned, as if it were a living entity, settling in for the night. Aria's eyelids grew heavy, and she found herself nodding off.

A sudden, loud bang jolted her awake. She sat up, heart pounding, and listened intently. The sound had come from somewhere in the castle, but she couldn't tell exactly where. She shook her head, trying to dispel the fog of sleep, and returned to her book. It was probably just the wind, she told herself. Old buildings made noises like that all the time.

As she continued reading, she became aware of another sound—soft, almost imperceptible whispers, like a breeze passing through the room. She looked around, but there was no one there. The hairs on the back of her neck stood up, and a chill ran down her spine. She strained to hear the words, but they were too faint to make out.

Deciding that it was time for bed, Aria closed the book and made her way back to her room. The hallways seemed darker and more oppressive than before, the shadows deeper and more menacing. She quickened her pace, eager to reach the safety of her bed.

As she reached her bedroom door, she heard another sound—soft footsteps echoing down the corridor. She turned, but there was no one there. Her heart raced, and she fumbled with the doorknob, desperate to get inside. Once she was in her room, she locked the door and leaned against it, trying to calm her racing heart.

"It's just your imagination," she whispered to herself. "You're letting this place get to you."

She changed into her pajamas and climbed into bed, pulling the covers up to her chin. The room was dark and quiet, the only light coming from the faint glow of the moon through the curtains. She closed her eyes, willing herself to sleep, but the whispers and footsteps continued to echo in her mind.

Sometime during the night, she was startled awake by a cold breeze that seemed to pass through the room. She sat up, looking around in confusion. The window was closed, and there was no draft. Her heart pounded as she listened for any signs of movement.

And then she saw it—a ghostly figure standing at the foot of her bed. It was a man, dressed in old-fashioned clothing, his face pale and sorrowful. His eyes were hollow and filled with an emotion Aria couldn't quite identify.

"Who are you?" she whispered, her voice trembling.

The figure didn't respond. Instead, it raised a hand, as if to beckon her. Aria's breath caught in her throat, and she felt a chill run through her body. She wanted to scream, to run, but she was frozen in place.

"Leave this place," the ghostly figure said, its voice echoing through the room. "You are not safe here."

And then, just as suddenly as it had appeared, the figure vanished, leaving Aria alone in the darkness. She sat there, shaking, for what felt like an eternity before finally collapsing back onto the bed. She pulled the covers over her head, her mind racing.

"Was that real?" she whispered to herself. "Or am I losing my mind?"

She lay awake for the rest of the night, too terrified to close her eyes. The whispers and footsteps continued, growing louder and more insistent. She could feel the presence of the ghostly figure, watching her, warning her.

By the time dawn broke, Aria was exhausted and on edge. She got up and dressed quickly, eager to find Lily and tell her what had happened. She made her way to Lily's room and knocked on the door.

"Lily, are you awake?"

The door opened, and Lily stood there, looking bleary-eyed and disheveled. "What's wrong, Aria? You look like you've seen a ghost."

"I think I have," Aria said, her voice shaking. "Can we talk?"

They went to the kitchen, where Mr. Blackwood was already preparing breakfast. He looked up as they entered, his expression concerned.

"Good morning, Miss Aria, Miss Lily. Is everything all right?"

Aria shook her head. "No, Mr. Blackwood. Something happened last night. I saw a ghost—a man. He told me to leave the castle."

Mr. Blackwood's expression grew serious. "I see. It seems you have encountered one of the castle's spirits."

"Who was he?" Aria asked. "Why did he tell me to leave?"

"I believe that was Lord William," Mr. Blackwood said. "He appears occasionally, warning visitors to leave. He is protecting the castle from some unknown threat."

"What kind of threat?" Lily asked, her eyes wide.

"No one knows for sure," Mr. Blackwood replied. "But the castle has a dark history, and there are many secrets yet to be uncovered."

Aria's mind raced as she tried to process what Mr. Blackwood was saying. "I need to know more," she said. "I need to understand what's happening here."

"I will help you in any way I can," Mr. Blackwood said. "But be cautious, Miss Aria. The spirits are not to be trifled with."

Aria nodded, determined to uncover the truth. She and Lily spent the day exploring the castle, searching for clues about Lord William and the castle's haunted past. They found more letters and journals, each one adding a piece to the puzzle.

As the day turned into evening, they decided to hold a séance to communicate with the spirits. They gathered candles, incense, and a crystal ball, and set up a circle in the library. As night fell, they lit the candles and sat in the circle, holding hands.

Mr. Blackwood began to chant, calling upon the spirits to join them. The air grew cold, and the flames flickered. Aria felt a chill run down her spine as the room filled with an eerie presence.

Suddenly, the crystal ball began to glow, and a misty figure appeared. It was Lord William, his eyes filled with sorrow.

"Who are you?" Mr. Blackwood asked.

"I am William Blackwood," the ghost replied, his voice echoing through the room. "I seek justice for my wife and myself. We were betrayed by my brother, Edward."

"We have proof," Aria said, holding up the journal. "Eleanor wrote about what happened. We can help you."

The ghost looked at the journal, his expression softening. "Thank you. You are brave to help us. But be warned, Edward's spirit is still here, and he will not let us go easily."

The room grew colder, and a dark, malevolent presence filled the air. Aria's heart pounded as she felt the anger and hatred emanating from the spirit of Edward.

"You will not escape," a voice hissed, filled with venom. "This castle is mine."

The candles flickered and went out, plunging the room into darkness. Aria felt a cold hand grasp her arm, and she screamed. The circle broke, and chaos ensued. Books flew off the shelves, and the furniture shook.

"Hold on!" Mr. Blackwood shouted, his voice barely audible over the commotion. "We must finish the séance!"

Aria struggled to stay focused, her mind racing. She reached out and grabbed the crystal ball, concentrating all her energy on the spirits of William and Eleanor.

"Leave us in peace!" she cried, her voice filled with determination. "You cannot keep them here forever!"

The room shook violently, and then, just as suddenly as it had started, the chaos stopped. The air grew still, and the dark presence dissipated. The candles relit themselves, casting a warm glow over the room.

Lord William and Eleanor appeared, their expressions filled with gratitude. "Thank you," William said. "You have freed us."

Aria felt a sense of relief wash over her. "What will happen now?"

"We will finally find peace," Eleanor said, her voice soft and serene. "The castle is yours now, to care for and protect."

With that, the spirits faded away, leaving Aria and Mr. Blackwood alone in the library. Aria felt a weight lift from her shoulders, knowing that she had done the right thing.

As dawn broke, she and Mr. Blackwood sat in the garden, reflecting on the events of the night. "You were brave," Mr. Blackwood said. "Not many would have faced the spirits so fearlessly."

Aria smiled. "I couldn't have done it without your help. Thank you."

"You have a strong spirit," Mr. Blackwood replied. "The castle is in good hands."

Aria looked out at the sunrise, feeling a sense of peace and belonging. She had inherited more than just a castle; she had inherited a legacy of courage and resilience. And she knew that, whatever challenges lay ahead, she was ready to face them.

Thus began Aria's journey at Blackwood Castle, a journey filled with mystery, adventure, and the promise of new beginnings.

For the first time since her arrival, Aria felt a sense of hope. She had faced the darkness and come out stronger. The whispers and footsteps might continue, but she knew she had allies in the spirits of William and Eleanor. The castle was her home now, and she was determined to uncover all its secrets, no matter how frightening.

As she and Mr. Blackwood finished their conversation and parted ways for the morning, Aria couldn't help but feel a renewed sense of purpose. She was ready to embrace her legacy and take on whatever the haunted castle had in store for her. The past was a part of her, and she was ready to face it head-on, with courage and determination.

And so, Aria's first night at Blackwood Castle, though filled with terror and uncertainty, also marked the beginning of a new chapter in her life—one of discovery, bravery, and the unraveling of long-buried secrets.

Chapter 4: The Castle's History

The dawn's first light seeped through the thick curtains of Aria's bedroom, casting long shadows across the room. Aria had slept restlessly, her mind plagued by the events of the previous night. The ghostly encounter and the unsettling séance left her with more questions than answers. Determined to uncover the mysteries of Blackwood Castle, she knew that delving into its history was the first step.

After a quick breakfast, Aria set off to explore the castle once more. This time, she was determined to find the hidden library that Mr. Blackwood had mentioned in passing. If the castle's dark secrets were recorded anywhere, it would be there.

Aria wandered through the labyrinthine corridors, her fingers tracing the intricate woodwork on the walls. The castle felt alive, as if it were watching her every move. She entered room after room, each filled with relics of the past—antique furniture, faded paintings, and ornate tapestries. But there was no sign of the hidden library.

Hours passed, and frustration began to set in. She was about to give up when she noticed something odd about a bookshelf in a small, dusty study. The books on one of the shelves were arranged differently, and there was a faint outline of a door behind them. Heart pounding with excitement, Aria pushed the shelf aside, revealing a hidden door.

With a deep breath, she pushed the door open and stepped inside. The room was dark, but as her eyes adjusted, she could make out rows upon rows of old books and journals. This was it—the hidden library. The air was thick with the smell of aged paper and leather, and a sense of reverence filled the room.

Aria found a lamp on a nearby table and lit it, casting a warm glow over the library. She took a moment to marvel at the sheer volume of knowledge contained within these walls. These books and journals held the key to understanding the castle's history and the curse that haunted it.

She started with the nearest shelf, pulling out a leather-bound journal with a faded title: **"The Chronicles of Blackwood Castle"**. The journal was written in an elegant script and dated back to the late 17th century. It began with the construction of the castle by Sir Thomas Blackwood, the patriarch of the Blackwood family.

"Sir Thomas Blackwood, a man of great ambition and wealth, commissioned the construction of Blackwood Castle in the year 1673. He envisioned a grand estate that would stand as a testament to his family's legacy for generations to come. The castle was built on the foundations of an ancient fortress, which some believed to be cursed."

ARIA READ ON, FASCINATED by the detailed accounts of the castle's early years. Sir Thomas was a shrewd and determined man, but his methods were often ruthless. He had made many enemies, and whispers of dark dealings and forbidden rituals began to circulate among the villagers.

As she continued reading, she came across an entry that made her blood run cold.

"In the year 1682, tragedy struck the Blackwood family. Sir Thomas's wife, Lady Eleanor, was found dead in her chambers, under mysterious circumstances. Her death was ruled a suicide, but many believed she had been murdered. Sir Thomas was inconsolable, and he became obsessed with finding the truth. His search led him down a dark path, and he began to dabble in the occult, seeking answers from beyond the grave."

ARIA PAUSED, HER MIND racing. This was the same Lady Eleanor whose ghost she had encountered during the séance. The journal continued, detailing Sir Thomas's descent into madness and the dark rituals he performed in an attempt to communicate with his deceased wife.

"Sir Thomas's obsession with the occult grew, and he began to

perform increasingly dangerous rituals. The castle became a place of fear and dread, as strange occurrences and ghostly apparitions plagued its halls. It was said that Sir Thomas had summoned something dark and malevolent, and the curse of Blackwood Castle was born."

ARIA CLOSED THE JOURNAL, her heart pounding. The origins of the curse were rooted in Sir Thomas's tragic loss and his desperate attempts to defy death. She set the journal aside and picked up another, this one from the 18th century.

The new journal was written by Sir Thomas's grandson, Edward Blackwood. It provided a chilling account of the castle's continuing descent into darkness.

"The curse of Blackwood Castle persisted through the generations. My father, William Blackwood, was a kind and just man, but even he could not escape the shadows that haunted our family. Ghosts of the past continued to plague us, and the castle's reputation as a place of death and despair grew."

EDWARD'S JOURNAL DETAILED numerous incidents of betrayal, murder, and madness within the Blackwood family. Each generation seemed to be cursed, their lives marked by tragedy and sorrow.

"In the year 1753, my brother, Richard, was found dead under suspicious circumstances. His death was ruled an accident, but I knew better. There was a darkness within the castle, a malevolent force that fed on our suffering. I have dedicated my life to uncovering the truth and breaking the curse, but it seems an impossible task."

ARIA FELT A DEEP SENSE of sorrow for the Blackwood family. The curse had torn them apart, generation after generation. She continued to read, uncovering more tales of betrayal and murder. One entry, in particular, caught her attention.

"In the year 1820, my ancestor, Elizabeth Blackwood, was

accused of witchcraft and executed by the villagers. She was a healer, a woman of great knowledge and power, but her abilities were misunderstood and feared. Her death marked a turning point in the curse, as the castle's spirits grew more restless and vengeful."

ARIA'S HEART ACHED for Elizabeth. She had been a victim of ignorance and fear, her death further fueling the castle's malevolent energy. Aria realized that the curse was not just a series of tragic events, but a cycle of fear, hatred, and despair that had been perpetuated over centuries.

Determined to break the curse, Aria continued to search through the library, seeking any clue that might help her. She came across a dusty, leather-bound book titled **"The Blackwood Grimoire."** The book was filled with spells and rituals, some of which were written in Latin and other ancient languages.

As she flipped through the pages, she found a section dedicated to summoning and banishing spirits. Her pulse quickened as she read the intricate instructions and symbols. This grimoire was a powerful tool, and it could be the key to freeing the spirits trapped within the castle.

Aria's thoughts were interrupted by a soft knock on the door. She looked up to see Mr. Blackwood standing in the doorway, a look of concern on his face.

"Miss Aria, I see you have found the hidden library," he said, stepping into the room.

"Yes, Mr. Blackwood. This place is incredible," Aria replied. "I've learned so much about the castle's history, but there is still so much I don't understand."

Mr. Blackwood nodded. "The history of Blackwood Castle is indeed dark and complex. The curse that plagues this place has its roots in the actions of our ancestors. But you must be careful, Miss Aria. Delving too deeply into the past can be dangerous."

"I need to understand what happened here," Aria said, her voice determined. "I need to find a way to break the curse and free the spirits."

Mr. Blackwood sighed, his expression troubled. "Very well. But you must promise me that you will proceed with caution. The spirits are powerful, and their anger can be unpredictable."

"I promise," Aria said, her resolve unwavering.

Mr. Blackwood joined her at the table, and together they continued to explore the library's contents. They found more journals, letters, and documents that provided a deeper understanding of the castle's history and the events that had led to the curse.

One journal, written by a servant named Margaret, offered a unique perspective on the Blackwood family. Margaret had served the family for decades, and her writings were filled with firsthand accounts of the strange occurrences and tragedies that had befallen the castle.

"The Blackwood family has always been shrouded in mystery and darkness. I have seen things that defy explanation—ghostly apparitions, unexplained noises, and objects moving on their own. The castle is alive with restless spirits, and the air is thick with sorrow and fear."

MARGARET'S JOURNAL detailed the lives of the Blackwood family members, their triumphs, and their tragedies. She wrote about the love and loss, the betrayals and murders that had shaped the family's history. Her words painted a vivid picture of a family cursed by their own actions and haunted by their past.

As Aria read Margaret's journal, she felt a deep sense of empathy for the Blackwood family. They had been victims of their own choices, trapped in a cycle of suffering that seemed impossible to break. But she also felt a glimmer of hope. If she could understand the source of the curse, perhaps she could find a way to end it.

She turned to Mr. Blackwood, her eyes filled with determination. "We need to find a way to break the curse," she said. "There must be something in these books that can help us."

Mr. Blackwood nodded. "The grimoire you found is a powerful tool. It contains spells and rituals that can summon and banish spirits. But using it is not without risk. The spirits are unpredictable, and their anger can be dangerous."

Aria took a deep breath, her mind racing. "I understand the risks, but we have to try. The spirits deserve to find peace, and the curse needs to be broken."

Mr. Blackwood looked at her with a mixture of admiration and concern. "Very well. We will do this together. But we must proceed with caution and respect for the spirits."

Aria spent the next several days poring over the grimoire, studying the spells and rituals with meticulous care. She learned about the different types of spirits, their strengths and weaknesses, and the methods for summoning and banishing them. She practiced the incantations and symbols, determined to get everything right.

Meanwhile, Mr. Blackwood continued to search through the library, seeking additional information that might help them. He found more journals and letters, each offering new insights into the castle's history and the curse that haunted it.

One letter, written by Sir Thomas Blackwood himself, provided a chilling account of his descent into madness.

"The death of my beloved Eleanor has left me shattered and broken. I have sought answers in the darkest corners of the earth, turning to forbidden rituals and ancient spells. I have summoned spirits from beyond the grave, seeking their knowledge and power. But with each summoning, the darkness grows stronger, and the curse tightens its grip on this castle."

SIR THOMAS'S LETTER detailed the rituals he had performed, the spirits he had summoned, and the consequences of his actions. It was clear that his obsession with the occult had unleashed a malevolent force that had cursed the Blackwood family for generations.

Aria and Mr. Blackwood knew that breaking the curse would not be easy, but they were determined to try. They prepared for the ritual, gathering the necessary ingredients and setting up the circle in the library. As night fell, they lit the candles and began the incantations.

The air grew cold, and the room filled with an eerie presence. The flames flickered, casting long shadows on the walls. Aria's heart pounded as she recited the incantation, her voice steady and clear.

"Spirits of Blackwood Castle, I summon thee. Come forth and hear my plea."

The crystal ball began to glow, and a misty figure appeared. It was Lord William, his eyes filled with sorrow.

"Why have you summoned me?" he asked, his voice echoing through the room.

"We seek to break the curse that plagues this castle," Aria replied. "We have learned of the dark rituals performed by Sir Thomas, and we wish to set the spirits free."

Lord William looked at her with a mixture of sadness and gratitude. "You are brave to undertake such a task. The curse is powerful, and the spirits are restless. But if you are determined, I will help you."

Aria and Mr. Blackwood continued the ritual, reciting the incantations and performing the necessary gestures. They felt the presence of other spirits in the room, their energy swirling around them.

"Spirits of Blackwood Castle, I command thee. Leave this place and find peace."

The room shook, and the air grew thick with tension. The spirits resisted, their anger and sorrow filling the space. But Aria and Mr. Blackwood remained steadfast, their voices strong and unwavering.

Finally, with a great surge of energy, the spirits began to dissipate. The room grew still, and the air cleared. Aria felt a sense of relief wash over her as the curse began to lift.

Lord William's figure faded, but not before he spoke one last time. "Thank you. You have freed us. The curse is broken, and the spirits can finally find peace."

Aria and Mr. Blackwood sat in silence, their hearts pounding with the realization of what they had accomplished. They had broken the curse that had plagued Blackwood Castle for centuries, freeing the spirits and bringing peace to the family.

As dawn broke, they stepped outside, feeling a sense of triumph and hope. The castle seemed lighter, as if a great weight had been lifted. The gardens sparkled in the morning light, and the air was filled with the sound of birdsong.

Aria knew that their journey was far from over. There were still mysteries to uncover, and the castle's history held many secrets yet to be revealed. But for now, she felt a sense of accomplishment and purpose.

She looked at Mr. Blackwood, her eyes filled with determination. "We did it," she said, her voice filled with emotion. "We broke the curse."

Mr. Blackwood nodded, a smile spreading across his face. "Yes, we did. And now, we can begin to rebuild and restore the castle to its former glory."

Aria felt a sense of excitement and possibility. The castle was her home now, and she was ready to embrace her legacy and take on whatever challenges lay ahead. With Mr. Blackwood by her side, she knew that they could accomplish anything.

Together, they would uncover the secrets of Blackwood Castle and ensure that its history was preserved for future generations. They would honor the spirits and the legacy of the Blackwood family, bringing light and hope to a place that had been shrouded in darkness for far too long.

Thus began a new chapter in Aria's life, one filled with mystery, adventure, and the promise of new beginnings. She had faced the darkness and emerged stronger, ready to embrace her destiny and the legacy of Blackwood Castle. The future was bright, and she was determined to make the most of it.

Chapter 5: The Phantom's Appearance

The first night Aria spent at Blackwood Castle was tumultuous, to say the least. She had seen and felt things that were beyond her comprehension. Determined to understand and solve the mysteries of her new home, she resolved to learn as much as possible about its history and the spirits trapped within its walls. But she was not prepared for what awaited her the following night.

After a day of exploration and research in the hidden library, Aria retired to her room, her mind buzzing with the stories she had uncovered. She had learned about Sir Thomas Blackwood's tragic descent into madness and the subsequent curse that had haunted the family for generations. Yet, there were still many gaps in the story—gaps she was determined to fill.

As the clock struck midnight, Aria found herself unable to sleep. The castle seemed to be alive with whispers and faint footsteps that echoed through the hallways. She lay in bed, her senses heightened, listening intently. Suddenly, the temperature in her room dropped, and a cold breeze brushed against her skin. She sat up, heart pounding, and saw the faint outline of a figure standing at the foot of her bed.

The figure became more distinct, revealing a tall man dressed in old-fashioned clothing. His face was pale and sorrowful, his eyes hollow with an expression of deep pain. Aria recognized him immediately—it was the same ghost she had seen the night before.

"Who are you?" she whispered, her voice trembling.

The ghost looked at her with a mix of sadness and urgency. "I am Lord William Blackwood," he replied, his voice echoing softly. "My soul is trapped in this castle, bound by betrayal and murder."

Aria's breath caught in her throat. "What happened to you?" she asked, her curiosity mingling with fear.

Lord William's ghost moved closer, his presence sending a chill through the room. "I was murdered by my brother, Edward, who coveted the inheritance that rightfully belonged to me. He betrayed me, and in his greed, he condemned my soul to wander these halls."

Aria's mind raced as she tried to process this revelation. She had read about the various tragedies that had befallen the Blackwood family, but hearing it directly from the ghost himself made it all the more real and horrifying.

"Why did he do it?" Aria asked, her voice barely above a whisper.

"Edward was always envious of my position and wealth," Lord William explained. "He believed that by killing me, he would secure his place as the head of the family. But his actions unleashed a curse upon this castle, trapping not only my soul but the souls of many others as well."

Aria felt a surge of anger on behalf of Lord William and the other spirits trapped in the castle. "There must be a way to set you free," she said determinedly. "I will help you."

Lord William's ghost looked at her with gratitude. "Thank you, Aria. But you must understand, this is no simple task. The curse is powerful, and Edward's spirit is still here, as malevolent as ever."

Aria nodded, her resolve unwavering. "I'm not afraid. Tell me what I need to do."

Lord William's ghost began to fade, his form becoming more translucent. "Seek the truth," he said, his voice growing faint. "Uncover the secrets of the past, and you will find a way to break the curse."

As the ghost disappeared, the room grew warmer, and the sense of foreboding lifted slightly. Aria sat in silence, her mind racing with the implications of what she had just learned. She knew that breaking the curse would be a monumental task, but she was determined to help the spirits find peace.

The next morning, Aria shared her encounter with Lily and Mr. Blackwood. They listened intently, their expressions serious.

"We need to uncover the truth about Edward's betrayal," Aria said. "There must be more information in the hidden library."

Mr. Blackwood nodded. "I will assist you in any way I can. The Blackwood family's history is complex, and there are many layers to uncover."

Together, they returned to the hidden library, determined to find the answers they sought. Aria felt a renewed sense of purpose as she sifted through the old books and journals, each one a potential key to unlocking the castle's dark past.

As they delved deeper into the library's contents, they found more references to Edward Blackwood. One journal, written by a servant named James, provided a chilling account of Edward's actions and his growing obsession with power.

"Edward Blackwood was a man consumed by envy and ambition. He despised his brother, William, and coveted the inheritance that was not his. I witnessed his descent into madness, as he plotted and schemed to eliminate his own blood. The night of the murder, I heard screams echoing through the halls, and I knew that Edward had finally carried out his wicked plan."

ARIA'S HEART ACHED for Lord William and the other victims of Edward's treachery. She knew that understanding the full extent of Edward's betrayal was crucial to breaking the curse. She continued to read, finding more accounts of Edward's cruelty and the fear he instilled in those around him.

"After William's death, Edward seized control of the estate, but his actions had dire consequences. The castle became a place of darkness and despair, haunted by the spirits of those who had been wronged. Edward himself was tormented by the very ghosts he had created, and he met a fitting end, driven to madness by his own guilt."

AS ARIA READ THESE words, she felt a strange mixture of relief and sorrow. Edward had paid for his crimes, but the curse he had unleashed continued to plague the castle. She knew that breaking the curse would require confronting Edward's spirit and putting an end to his malevolent influence once and for all.

Over the next few days, Aria, Lily, and Mr. Blackwood worked tirelessly to uncover more information about the curse and the rituals that could potentially break it. They found references to ancient spells and ceremonies, some of which were detailed in the Blackwood Grimoire.

Aria spent hours studying the grimoire, carefully memorizing the incantations and symbols. She knew that the ritual to banish Edward's spirit would be dangerous, but she was determined to succeed.

One evening, as they were poring over the books, Lily found a letter hidden between the pages of a journal. It was addressed to William from a woman named Eliza, who had been a close friend and confidante.

"My dearest William,

I write to you in great distress. Your brother, Edward, has become a danger to us all. His mind is consumed by dark thoughts, and I fear for your safety. You must be cautious, for I believe he intends to harm you. If anything should happen, know that I will do everything in my power to see that justice is served."

THE LETTER CONFIRMED what they had already suspected—Edward's intentions had been clear, even to those around him. Aria felt a renewed sense of urgency. She knew that they were close to uncovering the full truth, but there was still much work to be done.

That night, Aria returned to her room, her mind racing with thoughts of the upcoming ritual. She knew that confronting Edward's spirit would be dangerous, but she was determined to free Lord William and the other trapped souls.

As she lay in bed, she felt the temperature drop once more, and a cold breeze swept through the room. She sat up, her heart pounding, and saw Lord William's ghost standing at the foot of her bed.

"Aria," he said, his voice filled with urgency. "You are on the right path. But you must be careful. Edward's spirit is strong, and he will do everything in his power to stop you."

"I understand," Aria replied, her voice steady. "But I won't give up. We will break the curse and set you free."

Lord William's ghost looked at her with a mixture of gratitude and sadness. "Thank you, Aria. Your bravery gives me hope. But remember, the ritual must be performed with great care. Any mistake could have dire consequences."

Aria nodded, determined to succeed. "I will do everything I can to get it right."

As Lord William's ghost faded away, Aria felt a renewed sense of purpose. She knew that the task ahead would be difficult, but she was ready to face whatever challenges came her way.

The following morning, Aria, Lily, and Mr. Blackwood gathered in the hidden library to finalize their plans. They carefully reviewed the ritual, ensuring that they had all the necessary ingredients and understood the steps involved.

"We will perform the ritual in the grand ballroom," Mr. Blackwood said. "It is a large, open space, and the energy there is strong."

Aria nodded. "We need to make sure that everything is perfect. We can't afford any mistakes."

Lily looked at her friend with concern. "Are you sure about this, Aria? This is dangerous. We don't know what could happen."

"I'm sure," Aria replied, her voice firm. "We have to do this. We have to free the spirits and break the curse."

As night fell, they gathered their supplies and made their way to the grand ballroom. The room was vast and opulent, with high, vaulted ceilings and crystal chandeliers that sparkled in the dim light. They set up the ritual circle in the center of the room, arranging candles and incense around the perimeter.

Aria took a deep breath, her heart pounding with anticipation. She felt a mixture of fear and determination, knowing that this was their only chance to break the curse.

Mr. Blackwood began the incantation, his voice steady and clear. The air grew cold, and the flames of the candles flickered. Aria joined in, reciting the words she had memorized from the grimoire.

"Spirits of Blackwood Castle, I summon thee. Come forth and hear my plea."

The crystal ball in the center of the circle began to glow, and a misty figure appeared. It was Lord William, his eyes filled with sorrow and hope.

"Thank you for doing this," he said, his voice echoing through the room. "But be warned, Edward's spirit will not go quietly."

As if on cue, the room grew colder, and a dark, malevolent presence filled the air. Aria felt a chill run down her spine as she sensed Edward's spirit entering the room.

"You will not succeed," a voice hissed, filled with venom. "This castle is mine."

Aria steeled herself, her resolve unwavering. "We will break the curse, Edward. You cannot keep these spirits trapped forever."

The room shook violently, and the air grew thick with tension. The candles flickered and went out, plunging the room into darkness. Aria felt a cold hand grasp her arm, and she gasped in fear.

"Hold on!" Mr. Blackwood shouted, his voice barely audible over the commotion. "We must finish the ritual!"

Aria struggled to stay focused, her mind racing. She reached out and grabbed the crystal ball, concentrating all her energy on the spirits of William and Edward.

"Spirits of Blackwood Castle, I command thee. Leave this place and find peace."

The room shook again, and the dark presence grew stronger. Aria felt the malevolent energy swirling around her, threatening to overwhelm her. But she remained steadfast, her voice strong and unwavering.

"Leave us in peace, Edward. You cannot keep them here forever."

With a great surge of energy, the dark presence began to dissipate. The room grew still, and the air cleared. Aria felt a sense of relief wash over her as the curse began to lift.

Lord William's figure became more distinct, his expression filled with gratitude. "Thank you, Aria. You have freed us."

Aria felt tears welling up in her eyes. "What will happen now?"

"We will finally find peace," Lord William said, his voice soft and serene. "The curse is broken, and the spirits can move on."

As Lord William's ghost faded away, Aria felt a weight lift from her shoulders. She had done it. They had broken the curse and freed the spirits trapped within the castle.

As dawn broke, Aria, Lily, and Mr. Blackwood sat in the garden, reflecting on the events of the night. The castle seemed lighter, as if a great weight had been lifted. The gardens sparkled in the morning light, and the air was filled with the sound of birdsong.

"You were brave," Mr. Blackwood said, his voice filled with admiration. "Not many would have faced the spirits so fearlessly."

Aria smiled, feeling a sense of accomplishment. "I couldn't have done it without your help. Thank you."

"You have a strong spirit," Mr. Blackwood replied. "The castle is in good hands."

Aria looked out at the sunrise, feeling a sense of peace and belonging. She had inherited more than just a castle; she had inherited a legacy of courage and resilience. And she knew that, whatever challenges lay ahead, she was ready to face them.

Thus began a new chapter in Aria's life, one filled with mystery, adventure, and the promise of new beginnings. She had faced the darkness and emerged stronger, ready to embrace her destiny and the legacy of Blackwood Castle. The future was bright, and she was determined to make the most of it.

Chapter 6: The Hidden Passage

Aria woke to a golden morning, sunlight streaming through the curtains of her bedroom at Blackwood Castle. The air felt fresher, and there was a lightness to the castle that had been absent before. The successful banishing of Edward's spirit had lifted a significant weight from the ancient walls, but Aria knew there were still more secrets to uncover.

Over breakfast with Lily and Mr. Blackwood, Aria shared her thoughts. "We've come a long way, but I can't shake the feeling that there's more we need to understand about the curse. There might be other spirits still trapped, or perhaps there's another layer to the curse we haven't uncovered yet."

Lily nodded, her concern evident. "You're right, Aria. The castle's history is so tangled and dark. There might be hidden truths that could help us protect the castle and ourselves."

Mr. Blackwood, always the picture of calm and wisdom, agreed. "There are undoubtedly more secrets hidden within these walls. We must remain vigilant and continue our search."

Determined to leave no stone unturned, Aria spent the next few days exploring the castle's many rooms and corridors. She meticulously examined the architecture, the decor, and any unusual features that might hint at hidden passages or secret chambers. Her intuition told her that the key to fully understanding and breaking the curse lay somewhere within the castle's depths.

One afternoon, while wandering through a seldom-used wing of the castle, Aria noticed a peculiar tapestry depicting a battle scene from the Middle Ages. Unlike the other tapestries, this one seemed slightly newer and less worn. Her curiosity piqued, she examined it closely. As she ran her fingers along the edges, she felt a slight draft coming from behind it.

With a sense of anticipation, Aria carefully lifted the tapestry. Behind it, she found a narrow wooden door, almost invisible against the stone wall. Her heart raced as she pushed the door open, revealing a dark, winding staircase leading downward.

Aria hesitated for a moment, then called out, "Lily! Mr. Blackwood! Come here quickly!"

Within minutes, Lily and Mr. Blackwood arrived, their expressions a mix of curiosity and concern. Aria showed them the hidden door and the staircase.

"This could lead to something important," Aria said, her voice trembling with excitement. "We need to see where it goes."

Mr. Blackwood nodded. "I agree. But we must proceed with caution. There's no telling what we might find."

Aria took a deep breath and led the way, with Lily and Mr. Blackwood close behind. The staircase was narrow and steep, the air growing cooler and damper as they descended. Cobwebs brushed against their faces, and the sound of their footsteps echoed eerily in the confined space.

At the bottom of the staircase, they found themselves in a long, dimly lit corridor. The walls were lined with torches, which Aria lit one by one. The flickering light revealed ancient stone walls covered in moss and lichen. The air was thick with the scent of damp earth and decay.

They walked cautiously down the corridor, their senses on high alert. After several minutes, they reached a heavy wooden door, bound with iron and adorned with intricate carvings. Aria examined the door closely, noting the symbols and runes etched into the wood.

"These carvings are similar to those in the grimoire," she said, her voice filled with wonder. "This must be an important place."

Mr. Blackwood nodded. "Indeed. This door likely leads to an underground chamber. We must be prepared for anything."

With a deep breath, Aria pushed the door open. The hinges creaked, and the door swung open to reveal a vast underground chamber. The room was filled with an array of artifacts—ancient weapons, scrolls, and pottery—arranged on stone tables and shelves. In the center of the room stood a large stone altar, covered in strange symbols and markings.

Aria's eyes widened as she took in the sight. "This is incredible. It's like a hidden archive of the castle's history."

Lily nodded, her expression one of awe. "These artifacts could hold the key to understanding the curse."

They began to explore the chamber, examining the various artifacts and documents. Aria found a collection of scrolls written in an ancient language, while Lily discovered a series of paintings depicting scenes from the castle's history.

Mr. Blackwood focused on the altar, carefully studying the symbols and markings. "These runes are similar to those in the grimoire," he said, his voice thoughtful. "They appear to be part of a ritual or spell."

Aria joined him at the altar, her curiosity piqued. "Do you think these runes could help us break the curse?"

"It's possible," Mr. Blackwood replied. "We need to decipher their meaning and understand how they relate to the curse."

As they continued their exploration, Aria found a large, leather-bound book on a stone pedestal. The cover was adorned with intricate designs and symbols, similar to those on the altar. She carefully opened the book, revealing pages filled with handwritten notes and illustrations.

"This looks like a journal," Aria said, her excitement growing. "It might contain valuable information about the curse."

They gathered around the journal, eagerly reading the entries. The journal belonged to Sir Thomas Blackwood and detailed his experiments with the occult and his efforts to communicate with the spirits. The entries became increasingly desperate as he delved deeper into forbidden rituals, seeking to break the curse he had unwittingly unleashed.

One entry, in particular, caught Aria's attention.

"I have discovered a hidden passage beneath the castle, leading to an ancient chamber filled with artifacts of great power. Among these artifacts is a set of runes that hold the key to breaking the curse. But the rituals required are complex and dangerous. I must proceed with caution, for any mistake could have dire consequences."

ARIA'S HEART RACED as she read the entry. "This chamber must be the one Sir Thomas wrote about. These runes could be the key to breaking the curse."

Mr. Blackwood nodded. "Indeed. But we must be careful. The rituals are dangerous, and any mistake could have severe consequences."

Determined to proceed, Aria and Mr. Blackwood began to decipher the runes on the altar, cross-referencing them with the entries in Sir Thomas's journal. They worked late into the night, their focus unwavering. Lily assisted by organizing the artifacts and documents, ensuring that nothing was overlooked.

As they deciphered the runes, they discovered that the ritual required several specific ingredients and precise incantations. The process was intricate and demanding, requiring a deep understanding of the ancient symbols and their meanings.

"We need to gather these ingredients and prepare for the ritual," Mr. Blackwood said, his voice filled with determination. "But we must be careful. The spirits will likely resist our efforts, and any mistake could be disastrous."

Aria nodded, her resolve unwavering. "We've come this far. We can't turn back now."

Over the next few days, they gathered the necessary ingredients for the ritual, searching the castle and its grounds for rare herbs, crystals, and other items. The process was challenging, but their determination and teamwork paid off.

As they prepared for the ritual, Aria couldn't help but feel a sense of foreboding. The stakes were high, and the risks were great. But she knew that breaking the curse was the only way to bring peace to the castle and its restless spirits.

On the night of the ritual, they gathered in the underground chamber, their hearts pounding with anticipation. The air was thick with tension, and the flickering torchlight cast eerie shadows on the walls.

Aria stood at the altar, her hands steady as she arranged the ingredients and prepared the incantations. Mr. Blackwood stood beside her, his presence a source of strength and reassurance. Lily watched from the edge of the circle, her eyes filled with concern and hope.

"We are ready," Aria said, her voice steady. "Let's begin."

Mr. Blackwood nodded and began the incantation, his voice resonating through the chamber. Aria joined in, her voice clear and confident. The air grew colder, and the flames of the torches flickered as the ritual took hold.

"Spirits of Blackwood Castle, hear our plea," Mr. Blackwood intoned. "We seek to break the curse that binds you and bring you peace."

The crystal ball on the altar began to glow, and a misty figure appeared. It was Lord William, his eyes filled with sorrow and hope.

"Thank you for doing this," he said, his voice echoing through the chamber. "But be warned, the spirits will resist."

As if on cue, the chamber shook, and a dark, malevolent presence filled the air. Aria felt a chill run down her spine as she sensed Edward's spirit entering the room.

"You will not succeed," a voice hissed, filled with venom. "This curse is eternal."

Aria steeled herself, her resolve unwavering. "We will break the curse, Edward. You cannot keep these spirits trapped forever."

The chamber shook violently, and the air grew thick with tension. The torches flickered and went out, plunging the room into darkness. Aria felt a cold hand grasp her arm, and she gasped in fear.

"Hold on!" Mr. Blackwood shouted, his voice barely audible over the commotion. "We must finish the ritual!"

Aria struggled to stay focused, her mind racing. She reached out and grabbed the crystal ball, concentrating all her energy on the spirits of William and Edward.

"Spirits of Blackwood Castle, I command thee. Leave this place and find peace."

The chamber shook again, and the dark presence grew stronger. Aria felt the malevolent energy swirling around her, threatening to overwhelm her. But she remained steadfast, her voice strong and unwavering.

"Leave us in peace, Edward. You cannot keep them here forever."

With a great surge of energy, the dark presence began to dissipate. The room grew still, and the air cleared. Aria felt a sense of relief wash over her as the curse began to lift.

Lord William's figure became more distinct, his expression filled with gratitude. "Thank you, Aria. You have freed us."

Aria felt tears welling up in her eyes. "What will happen now?"

"We will finally find peace," Lord William said, his voice soft and serene. "The curse is broken, and the spirits can move on."

As Lord William's ghost faded away, Aria felt a weight lift from her shoulders. She had done it. They had broken the curse and freed the spirits trapped within the castle.

As dawn broke, Aria, Lily, and Mr. Blackwood sat in the garden, reflecting on the events of the night. The castle seemed lighter, as if a great weight had been lifted. The gardens sparkled in the morning light, and the air was filled with the sound of birdsong.

"You were brave," Mr. Blackwood said, his voice filled with admiration. "Not many would have faced the spirits so fearlessly."

Aria smiled, feeling a sense of accomplishment. "I couldn't have done it without your help. Thank you."

"You have a strong spirit," Mr. Blackwood replied. "The castle is in good hands."

Aria looked out at the sunrise, feeling a sense of peace and belonging. She had inherited more than just a castle; she had inherited a legacy of courage and resilience. And she knew that, whatever challenges lay ahead, she was ready to face them.

Thus began a new chapter in Aria's life, one filled with mystery, adventure, and the promise of new beginnings. She had faced the darkness and emerged stronger, ready to embrace her destiny and the legacy of Blackwood Castle. The future was bright, and she was determined to make the most of it.

Over the following weeks, Aria, Lily, and Mr. Blackwood continued to explore the hidden chamber, cataloging the artifacts and documents they found. They discovered more about the castle's history and the lives of the Blackwood family members who had lived and died within its walls.

One particularly intriguing find was a series of letters between Sir Thomas Blackwood and a mysterious figure known only as "The Alchemist." These letters detailed their collaboration on various experiments and rituals, many of which were aimed at uncovering the secrets of life and death.

"My dear Alchemist,

I have made significant progress in our quest for knowledge. The hidden chamber beneath the castle has yielded many valuable artifacts, and I believe we are close to uncovering the

key to eternal life. However, the risks are great, and I must proceed with caution. The spirits grow restless, and I fear that our actions may have unintended consequences."

THE LETTERS PROVIDED a fascinating glimpse into Sir Thomas's mind and his obsession with the occult. They also hinted at the possibility that there were still more hidden chambers and passages within the castle, waiting to be discovered.

Aria felt a renewed sense of purpose as she delved deeper into the castle's history. She was determined to uncover all of its secrets and ensure that the spirits of the Blackwood family could finally find peace.

One evening, as they were exploring the hidden chamber, Aria noticed a loose stone in the wall near the altar. She carefully pried it open, revealing a small, dark passageway. Her heart raced with excitement as she peered inside.

"Look at this," she said, her voice filled with wonder. "There's another passageway behind this wall."

Mr. Blackwood examined the passageway, his expression thoughtful. "This could lead to another hidden chamber. We should investigate."

Aria, Mr. Blackwood, and Lily entered the passageway, their torches casting eerie shadows on the walls. The air was damp and musty, and the narrow corridor seemed to stretch on forever. After several minutes of walking, they reached a heavy wooden door, similar to the one they had found earlier.

Aria pushed the door open, revealing another underground chamber. This one was smaller than the first, but it was filled with even more artifacts and documents. In the center of the room stood a large, ornate chest, its surface covered in intricate carvings and symbols.

"This must be the Alchemist's chamber," Mr. Blackwood said, his voice filled with awe. "These artifacts are incredibly valuable."

Aria approached the chest, her heart pounding with anticipation. She carefully opened it, revealing a collection of ancient books, scrolls, and vials filled with strange liquids.

"These are the Alchemist's writings," she said, her voice trembling with excitement. "They could contain the key to understanding the curse and the rituals Sir Thomas performed."

They spent hours examining the contents of the chest, reading through the Alchemist's notes and experimenting with the various vials and potions. The writings detailed complex alchemical processes and rituals, many of which were aimed at achieving immortality and communicating with the spirit world.

One book, in particular, caught Aria's attention. It was a large, leather-bound volume titled **"The Alchemist's Grimoire."** The book contained detailed instructions for a powerful ritual that could potentially break the curse and free the spirits trapped within the castle.

"This is it," Aria said, her voice filled with excitement. "This grimoire contains the ritual we need."

Mr. Blackwood examined the book, his expression serious. "This ritual is incredibly complex and dangerous. We must proceed with the utmost caution."

Aria nodded, her resolve unwavering. "We've come this far. We can't turn back now."

Over the next few days, they prepared for the ritual, gathering the necessary ingredients and studying the incantations and symbols. They knew that this would be their final attempt to break the curse, and they were determined to succeed.

On the night of the ritual, they gathered in the Alchemist's chamber, their hearts pounding with anticipation. The air was thick with tension, and the flickering torchlight cast eerie shadows on the walls.

Aria stood at the altar, her hands steady as she arranged the ingredients and prepared the incantations. Mr. Blackwood stood beside her, his presence a source of strength and reassurance. Lily watched from the edge of the circle, her eyes filled with concern and hope.

"We are ready," Aria said, her voice steady. "Let's begin."

Mr. Blackwood nodded and began the incantation, his voice resonating through the chamber. Aria joined in, her voice clear and confident. The air grew colder, and the flames of the torches flickered as the ritual took hold.

"Spirits of Blackwood Castle, I summon thee. Come forth and hear my plea."

The crystal ball on the altar began to glow, and a misty figure appeared. It was Lord William, his eyes filled with sorrow and hope.

"Thank you for doing this," he said, his voice echoing through the chamber. "But be warned, the spirits will resist."

As if on cue, the chamber shook, and a dark, malevolent presence filled the air. Aria felt a chill run down her spine as she sensed Edward's spirit entering the room.

"You will not succeed," a voice hissed, filled with venom. "This curse is eternal."

Aria steeled herself, her resolve unwavering. "We will break the curse, Edward. You cannot keep these spirits trapped forever."

The chamber shook violently, and the air grew thick with tension. The torches flickered and went out, plunging the room into darkness. Aria felt a cold hand grasp her arm, and she gasped in fear.

"Hold on!" Mr. Blackwood shouted, his voice barely audible over the commotion. "We must finish the ritual!"

Aria struggled to stay focused, her mind racing. She reached out and grabbed the crystal ball, concentrating all her energy on the spirits of William and Edward.

"Spirits of Blackwood Castle, I command thee. Leave this place and find peace."

The chamber shook again, and the dark presence grew stronger. Aria felt the malevolent energy swirling around her, threatening to overwhelm her. But she remained steadfast, her voice strong and unwavering.

"Leave us in peace, Edward. You cannot keep them here forever."

With a great surge of energy, the dark presence began to dissipate. The room grew still, and the air cleared. Aria felt a sense of relief wash over her as the curse began to lift.

Lord William's figure became more distinct, his expression filled with gratitude. "Thank you, Aria. You have freed us."

Aria felt tears welling up in her eyes. "What will happen now?"

"We will finally find peace," Lord William said, his voice soft and serene. "The curse is broken, and the spirits can move on."

As Lord William's ghost faded away, Aria felt a weight lift from her shoulders. She had done it. They had broken the curse and freed the spirits trapped within the castle.

As dawn broke, Aria, Lily, and Mr. Blackwood sat in the garden, reflecting on the events of the night. The castle seemed lighter, as if a great weight had been lifted. The gardens sparkled in the morning light, and the air was filled with the sound of birdsong.

"You were brave," Mr. Blackwood said, his voice filled with admiration. "Not many would have faced the spirits so fearlessly."

Aria smiled, feeling a sense of accomplishment. "I couldn't have done it without your help. Thank you."

"You have a strong spirit,"

Mr. Blackwood replied. "The castle is in good hands."

Aria looked out at the sunrise, feeling a sense of peace and belonging. She had inherited more than just a castle; she had inherited a legacy of courage and resilience. And she knew that, whatever challenges lay ahead, she was ready to face them.

Thus began a new chapter in Aria's life, one filled with mystery, adventure, and the promise of new beginnings. She had faced the darkness and emerged stronger, ready to embrace her destiny and the legacy of Blackwood Castle. The future was bright, and she was determined to make the most of it.

Over the following weeks, Aria, Lily, and Mr. Blackwood continued to explore the hidden chambers, cataloging the artifacts and documents they found. They discovered more about the castle's history and the lives of the Blackwood family members who had lived and died within its walls.

One particularly intriguing find was a series of letters between Sir Thomas Blackwood and a mysterious figure known only as "The Alchemist." These letters detailed their collaboration on various experiments and rituals, many of which were aimed at uncovering the secrets of life and death.

"My dear Alchemist,

I have made significant progress in our quest for knowledge. The hidden chamber beneath the castle has yielded many valuable artifacts, and I believe we are close to uncovering the key to eternal life. However, the risks are great, and I must proceed with caution. The spirits grow restless, and I fear that our actions may have unintended consequences."

The letters provided a fascinating glimpse into Sir Thomas's mind and his obsession with the occult. They also hinted at the possibility that there were still more hidden chambers and passages within the castle, waiting to be discovered.

Aria felt a renewed sense of purpose as she delved deeper into the castle's history. She was determined to uncover all of its secrets and ensure that the spirits of the Blackwood family could finally find peace.

One evening, as they were exploring the hidden chamber, Aria noticed a loose stone in the wall near the altar. She carefully pried it open, revealing a small, dark passageway. Her heart raced with excitement as she peered inside.

"Look at this," she said, her voice filled with wonder. "There's another passageway behind this wall."

Mr. Blackwood examined the passageway, his expression thoughtful. "This could lead to another hidden chamber. We should investigate."

Aria, Mr. Blackwood, and Lily entered the passageway, their torches casting eerie shadows on the walls. The air was damp and musty, and the narrow corridor seemed to stretch on forever. After several minutes of walking, they reached a heavy wooden door, similar to the one they had found earlier.

Aria pushed the door open, revealing another underground chamber. This one was smaller than the first, but it was filled with even more artifacts and documents. In the center of the room stood a large, ornate chest, its surface covered in intricate carvings and symbols.

"This must be the Alchemist's chamber," Mr. Blackwood said, his voice filled with awe. "These artifacts are incredibly valuable."

Aria approached the chest, her heart pounding with anticipation. She carefully opened it, revealing a collection of ancient books, scrolls, and vials filled with strange liquids.

"These are the Alchemist's writings," she said, her voice trembling with excitement. "They could contain the key to understanding the curse and the rituals Sir Thomas performed."

They spent hours examining the contents of the chest, reading through the Alchemist's notes and experimenting with the various vials and potions. The writings detailed complex alchemical processes and rituals, many of which were aimed at achieving immortality and communicating with the spirit world.

One book, in particular, caught Aria's attention. It was a large, leather-bound volume titled "The Alchemist's Grimoire." The book contained detailed instructions for a powerful ritual that could potentially break the curse and free the spirits trapped within the castle.

"This is it," Aria said, her voice filled with excitement. "This grimoire contains the ritual we need."

Mr. Blackwood examined the book, his expression serious. "This ritual is incredibly complex and dangerous. We must proceed with the utmost caution."

Aria nodded, her resolve unwavering. "We've come this far. We can't turn back now."

Over the next few days, they prepared for the ritual, gathering the necessary ingredients and studying the incantations and symbols. They knew that this would be their final attempt to break the curse, and they were determined to succeed.

On the night of the ritual, they gathered in the Alchemist's chamber, their hearts pounding with anticipation. The air was thick with tension, and the flickering torchlight cast eerie shadows on the walls.

Aria stood at the altar, her hands steady as she arranged the ingredients and prepared the incantations. Mr. Blackwood stood beside her, his presence a source of strength and reassurance. Lily watched from the edge of the circle, her eyes filled with concern and hope.

"We are ready," Aria said, her voice steady. "Let's begin."

Mr. Blackwood nodded and began the incantation, his voice resonating through the chamber. Aria joined in, her voice clear and confident. The air grew colder, and the flames of the torches flickered as the ritual took hold.

"Spirits of Blackwood Castle, I summon thee. Come forth and hear my plea."

The crystal ball on the altar began to glow, and a misty figure appeared. It was Lord William, his eyes filled with sorrow and hope.

"Thank you for doing this," he said, his voice echoing through the chamber. "But be warned, the spirits will resist."

As if on cue, the chamber shook, and a dark, malevolent presence filled the air. Aria felt a chill run down her spine as she sensed Edward's spirit entering the room.

"You will not succeed," a voice hissed, filled with venom. "This curse is eternal."

Aria steeled herself, her resolve unwavering. "We will break the curse, Edward. You cannot keep these spirits trapped forever."

The chamber shook violently, and the air grew thick with tension. The torches flickered and went out, plunging the room into darkness. Aria felt a cold hand grasp her arm, and she gasped in fear.

"Hold on!" Mr. Blackwood shouted, his voice barely audible over the commotion. "We must finish the ritual!"

Aria struggled to stay focused, her mind racing. She reached out and grabbed the crystal ball, concentrating all her energy on the spirits of William and Edward.

"Spirits of Blackwood Castle, I command thee. Leave this place and find peace."

The chamber shook again, and the dark presence grew stronger. Aria felt the malevolent energy swirling around her, threatening to overwhelm her. But she remained steadfast, her voice strong and unwavering.

"Leave us in peace, Edward. You cannot keep them here forever."

With a great surge of energy, the dark presence began to dissipate. The room grew still, and the air cleared. Aria felt a sense of relief wash over her as the curse began to lift.

Lord William's figure became more distinct, his expression filled with gratitude. "Thank you, Aria. You have freed us."

Aria felt tears welling up in her eyes. "What will happen now?"

"We will finally find peace," Lord William said, his voice soft and serene. "The curse is broken, and the spirits can move on."

As Lord William's ghost faded away, Aria felt a weight lift from her shoulders. She had done it. They had broken the curse and freed the spirits trapped within the castle.

As dawn broke, Aria, Lily, and Mr. Blackwood sat in the garden, reflecting on the events of the night. The castle seemed lighter, as if a great weight had been lifted. The gardens sparkled in the morning light, and the air was filled with the sound of birdsong.

"You were brave," Mr. Blackwood said, his voice filled with admiration. "Not many would have faced the spirits so fearlessly."

Aria smiled, feeling a sense of accomplishment. "I couldn't have done it without your help. Thank you."

"You have a strong spirit," Mr. Blackwood replied. "The castle is in good hands."

Aria looked out at the sunrise, feeling a sense of peace and belonging. She had inherited more than just a castle; she had inherited a legacy of courage and resilience. And she knew that, whatever challenges lay ahead, she was ready to face them.

Thus began a new chapter in Aria's life, one filled with mystery, adventure, and the promise of new beginnings. She had faced the darkness and emerged stronger, ready to embrace her destiny and the legacy of Blackwood Castle. The future was bright, and she was determined to make the most of it.

Chapter 7: The Curse Unveiled

Aria awoke to the soft light of dawn filtering through the heavy curtains of her bedroom at Blackwood Castle. The events of the past few days had left her mentally and emotionally drained, but there was a sense of purpose that now propelled her forward. The curse was real, and its weight could be felt in every corner of the castle. Determined to uncover the truth and bring justice to Lord William's spirit, Aria knew her journey was far from over.

After a quick breakfast, Aria, Lily, and Mr. Blackwood gathered in the library to discuss their next steps. The hidden chamber and the artifacts they had discovered were only part of the puzzle. To break the curse, they needed to understand the full story of Lord William's death and the events that led to the curse being placed on the castle.

"We need to find more information about Edward and his betrayal," Aria said, her voice resolute. "We have to piece together the truth behind Lord William's death."

Lily nodded in agreement. "We should start with the journals and letters we found in the hidden chamber. There must be something we've missed."

Mr. Blackwood added, "I also suggest we explore areas of the castle we haven't yet investigated. There could be more hidden passages and chambers that hold the answers we seek."

The trio set to work, each taking a different section of the library. Aria focused on the journals, carefully reading each entry for any mention of Edward and his actions leading up to Lord William's death. She found several references to Edward's growing envy and ambition, but the details were frustratingly vague.

As the hours passed, Aria's frustration grew. The pieces of the puzzle were there, but they were scattered and incomplete. Just as she was about to take a break, she noticed a small, leather-bound journal tucked away on a high shelf. The cover was worn, and the pages were yellowed with age. It looked older than the other journals she had examined.

Aria carefully took the journal down and opened it. The handwriting was delicate and neat, and the entries were dated from the early 1700s. As she read, she realized it was the diary of Lady Eleanor, Lord William's wife.

"March 15, 1712: William and I have been married for five years now, and our love grows stronger with each passing day. However, I worry about his brother, Edward. There is a darkness in him that frightens me. He is envious of William's position and wealth, and I fear he may do something terrible."

ARIA'S HEART RACED as she read Lady Eleanor's words. This diary could provide the key to understanding Edward's motives and the events that led to the curse. She continued reading, finding entries that described Edward's increasingly erratic behavior and his growing obsession with taking control of the estate.

"June 21, 1713: Edward has become more aggressive in his pursuit of power. He constantly argues with William, accusing him of stealing what is rightfully his. William tries to reason with him, but it is clear that Edward's jealousy has consumed him. I fear for our safety."

AS ARIA DELVED DEEPER into the diary, she found entries that detailed Edward's sinister plans.

"September 9, 1713: I overheard Edward speaking with one of the servants today. He spoke of a plan to remove William from his position permanently. I am terrified of what he might do. I must warn William and protect our family."

ARIA'S HANDS TREMBLED as she read the final entries in the diary.

"October 31, 1713: William is dead. Edward has done the unthinkable. He poisoned William's wine during a family dinner. I saw him do it, but it was too late to stop him.

William's death was ruled a tragic accident, but I know the truth. I must find a way to expose Edward and bring justice to William's spirit."

THE DIARY ENDED ABRUPTLY, leaving Aria with a heavy heart. Lady Eleanor had known the truth but had been unable to stop Edward or bring him to justice. Now it was up to Aria to finish what Lady Eleanor had started.

Aria shared her findings with Lily and Mr. Blackwood. They were shocked and saddened by the revelation but also determined to use this new information to break the curse.

"We need to find evidence that can prove Edward's guilt," Aria said. "Something that can bring closure to William's spirit and lift the curse."

Mr. Blackwood suggested, "There may be more hidden chambers in the castle where evidence could be hidden. We should continue our search."

With renewed determination, they explored the castle further, examining every nook and cranny for hidden passages and secret rooms. The increasing supernatural activity—strange noises, cold drafts, and flickering lights—only served to heighten their sense of urgency.

One evening, as they were investigating a rarely used wing of the castle, Aria noticed an old, faded tapestry hanging on the wall. The tapestry depicted a hunting scene, but something about it seemed off. She carefully lifted the edge and discovered a hidden door behind it.

"Look at this," she called to Lily and Mr. Blackwood. "Another hidden passage."

They opened the door and found themselves in a narrow corridor that led to a small, dusty room. Inside, they discovered a chest filled with old documents and personal belongings.

Aria carefully examined the contents of the chest, her heart pounding with anticipation. Among the documents, she found a letter addressed to Edward from an unknown sender. The letter confirmed Edward's involvement in William's death and revealed the extent of his treachery.

"Edward,

The plan is in place. The poison will be administered during the family dinner. Once William is out of the way, you will

take control of the estate. Remember, our agreement stands. Do not fail me."

THE LETTER WAS SIGNED with a symbol that Aria recognized from the Alchemist's Grimoire. It was the mark of a secret society that had been involved in dark rituals and forbidden practices.

"This is it," Aria said, her voice trembling. "This letter proves Edward's guilt. We need to use this to bring justice to William's spirit."

Mr. Blackwood nodded. "We must perform a ritual to summon William's spirit and present this evidence. It may be the key to lifting the curse."

They prepared for the ritual, gathering the necessary ingredients and setting up the circle in the hidden chamber. As night fell, they lit the candles and began the incantations.

"Spirits of Blackwood Castle, I summon thee. Come forth and hear our plea."

The crystal ball on the altar began to glow, and a misty figure appeared. It was Lord William, his eyes filled with sorrow and hope.

"Thank you for doing this," he said, his voice echoing through the chamber. "But be warned, the spirits will resist."

As if on cue, the chamber shook, and a dark, malevolent presence filled the air. Aria felt a chill run down her spine as she sensed Edward's spirit entering the room.

"You will not succeed," a voice hissed, filled with venom. "This curse is eternal."

Aria steeled herself, her resolve unwavering. "We will break the curse, Edward. You cannot keep these spirits trapped forever."

The chamber shook violently, and the air grew thick with tension. The torches flickered and went out, plunging the room into darkness. Aria felt a cold hand grasp her arm, and she gasped in fear.

"Hold on!" Mr. Blackwood shouted, his voice barely audible over the commotion. "We must finish the ritual!"

Aria struggled to stay focused, her mind racing. She reached out and grabbed the crystal ball, concentrating all her energy on the spirits of William and Edward.

"Spirits of Blackwood Castle, I command thee. Leave this place and find peace."

The chamber shook again, and the dark presence grew stronger. Aria felt the malevolent energy swirling around her, threatening to overwhelm her. But she remained steadfast, her voice strong and unwavering.

"Leave us in peace, Edward. You cannot keep them here forever."

With a great surge of energy, the dark presence began to dissipate. The room grew still, and the air cleared. Aria felt a sense of relief wash over her as the curse began to lift.

Lord William's figure became more distinct, his expression filled with gratitude. "Thank you, Aria. You have freed us."

Aria felt tears welling up in her eyes. "What will happen now?"

"We will finally find peace," Lord William said, his voice soft and serene. "The curse is broken, and the spirits can move on."

As Lord William's ghost faded away, Aria felt a weight lift from her shoulders. She had done it. They had broken the curse and freed the spirits trapped within the castle.

As dawn broke, Aria, Lily, and Mr. Blackwood sat in the garden, reflecting on the events of the night. The castle seemed lighter, as if a great weight had been lifted. The gardens sparkled in the morning light, and the air was filled with the sound of birdsong.

"You were brave," Mr. Blackwood said, his voice filled with admiration. "Not many would have faced the spirits so fearlessly."

Aria smiled, feeling a sense of accomplishment. "I couldn't have done it without your help. Thank you."

"You have a strong spirit," Mr. Blackwood replied. "The castle is in good hands."

Aria looked out at the sunrise, feeling a sense of peace and belonging. She had inherited more than just a castle; she had inherited a legacy of courage and resilience. And she knew that, whatever challenges lay ahead, she was ready to face them.

Thus began a new chapter in Aria's life, one filled with mystery, adventure, and the promise of new beginnings. She had faced the darkness and emerged stronger, ready to embrace her destiny and the legacy of Blackwood Castle. The future was bright, and she was determined to make the most of it.

Over the following weeks, Aria, Lily, and Mr. Blackwood continued to explore the hidden chambers, cataloging the artifacts and documents they found. They discovered more about the castle's history and the lives of the Blackwood family members who had lived and died within its walls.

One particularly intriguing find was a series of letters between Sir Thomas Blackwood and a mysterious figure known only as "The Alchemist." These letters detailed their collaboration on various experiments and rituals, many of which were aimed at uncovering the secrets of life and death.

"My dear Alchemist,

I have made significant progress in our quest for knowledge. The hidden chamber beneath the castle has yielded many valuable artifacts, and I believe we are close to uncovering the key to eternal life. However, the risks are great, and I must proceed with caution. The spirits grow restless, and I fear that our actions may have unintended consequences."

THE LETTERS PROVIDED a fascinating glimpse into Sir Thomas's mind and his obsession with the occult. They also hinted at the possibility that there were still more hidden chambers and passages within the castle, waiting to be discovered.

Aria felt a renewed sense of purpose as she delved deeper into the castle's history. She was determined to uncover all of its secrets and ensure that the spirits of the Blackwood family could finally find peace.

One evening, as they were exploring the hidden chamber, Aria noticed a loose stone in the wall near the altar. She carefully pried it open, revealing a small, dark passageway. Her heart raced with excitement as she peered inside.

"Look at this," she said, her voice filled with wonder. "There's another passageway behind this wall."

Mr. Blackwood examined the passageway, his expression thoughtful. "This could lead to another hidden chamber. We should investigate."

Aria, Mr. Blackwood, and Lily entered the passageway, their torches casting eerie shadows on the walls. The air was damp and musty, and the narrow corridor seemed to stretch on forever. After several minutes of walking, they reached a heavy wooden door, similar to the one they had found earlier.

Aria pushed the door open, revealing another underground chamber. This one was smaller than the first, but it was filled with even more artifacts and documents. In the center of the room stood a large, ornate chest, its surface covered in intricate carvings and symbols.

"This must be the Alchemist's chamber," Mr. Blackwood said, his voice filled with awe. "These artifacts are incredibly valuable."

Aria approached the chest, her heart pounding with anticipation. She carefully opened it, revealing a collection of ancient books, scrolls, and vials filled with strange liquids.

"These are the Alchemist's writings," she said, her voice trembling with excitement. "They could contain the key to understanding the curse and the rituals Sir Thomas performed."

They spent hours examining the contents of the chest, reading through the Alchemist's notes and experimenting with the various vials and potions. The writings detailed complex alchemical processes and rituals, many of which were aimed at achieving immortality and communicating with the spirit world.

One book, in particular, caught Aria's attention. It was a large, leather-bound volume titled **"The Alchemist's Grimoire."** The book contained detailed instructions for a powerful ritual that could potentially break the curse and free the spirits trapped within the castle.

"This is it," Aria said, her voice filled with excitement. "This grimoire contains the ritual we need."

Mr. Blackwood examined the book, his expression serious. "This ritual is incredibly complex and dangerous. We must proceed with the utmost caution."

Aria nodded, her resolve unwavering. "We've come this far. We can't turn back now."

Over the next few days, they prepared for the ritual, gathering the necessary ingredients and studying the incantations and symbols. They knew that this would be their final attempt to break the curse, and they were determined to succeed.

On the night of the ritual, they gathered in the Alchemist's chamber, their hearts pounding with anticipation. The air was thick with tension, and the flickering torchlight cast eerie shadows on the walls.

Aria stood at the altar, her hands steady as she arranged the ingredients and prepared the incantations. Mr. Blackwood stood beside her, his presence a source of strength and reassurance. Lily watched from the edge of the circle, her eyes filled with concern and hope.

"We are ready," Aria said, her voice steady. "Let's begin."

Mr. Blackwood nodded and began the incantation, his voice resonating through the chamber. Aria joined in, her voice clear and confident. The air grew colder, and the flames of the torches flickered as the ritual took hold.

"Spirits of Blackwood Castle, I summon thee. Come forth and hear my plea."

The crystal ball on the altar began to glow, and a misty figure appeared. It was Lord William, his eyes filled with sorrow and hope.

"Thank you for doing this," he said, his voice echoing through the chamber. "But be warned, the spirits will resist."

As if on cue, the chamber shook, and a dark, malevolent presence filled the air. Aria felt a chill run down her spine as she sensed Edward's spirit entering the room.

"You will not succeed," a voice hissed, filled with venom. "This curse is eternal."

Aria steeled herself, her resolve unwavering. "We will break the curse, Edward. You cannot keep these spirits trapped forever."

The chamber shook violently, and the air grew thick with tension. The torches flickered and went out, plunging the room into darkness. Aria felt a cold hand grasp her arm, and she gasped in fear.

"Hold on!" Mr. Blackwood shouted, his voice barely audible over the commotion. "We must finish the ritual!"

Aria struggled to stay focused, her mind racing. She reached out and grabbed the crystal ball, concentrating all her energy on the spirits of William and Edward.

"Spirits of Blackwood Castle, I command thee. Leave this place and find peace."

The chamber shook again, and the dark presence grew stronger. Aria felt the malevolent energy swirling around her, threatening to overwhelm her. But she remained steadfast, her voice strong and unwavering.

"Leave us in peace, Edward. You cannot keep them here forever."

With a great surge of energy, the dark presence began to dissipate. The room grew still, and the air cleared. Aria felt a sense of relief wash over her as the curse began to lift.

Lord William's figure became more distinct, his expression filled with gratitude. "Thank you, Aria. You have freed us."

Aria felt tears welling up in her eyes. "What will happen now?"

"We will finally find peace," Lord William said, his voice soft and serene. "The curse is broken, and the spirits can move on."

As Lord William's ghost faded away, Aria felt a weight lift from her shoulders. She had done it. They had broken the curse and freed the spirits trapped within the castle.

As dawn broke, Aria, Lily, and Mr. Blackwood sat in the garden, reflecting on the events of the night. The castle seemed lighter, as if a great weight had been lifted. The gardens sparkled in the morning light, and the air was filled with the sound of birdsong.

"You were brave," Mr. Blackwood said, his voice filled with admiration. "Not many would have faced the spirits so fearlessly."

Aria smiled, feeling a sense of accomplishment. "I couldn't have done it without your help. Thank you."

"You have a strong spirit," Mr. Blackwood replied. "The castle is in good hands."

Aria looked out at the sunrise, feeling a sense of peace and belonging. She had inherited more than just a castle; she had inherited a legacy of courage and resilience. And she knew that, whatever challenges lay ahead, she was ready to face them.

Thus began a new chapter in Aria's life, one filled with mystery, adventure, and the promise of new beginnings. She had faced the darkness and emerged stronger, ready to embrace her destiny and the legacy of Blackwood Castle. The future was bright, and she was determined to make the most of it.

Chapter 8: Allies in the Shadows

The days following the lifting of the initial curse brought a strange calm to Blackwood Castle. The air felt lighter, the shadows less oppressive, but Aria knew that not all spirits had been set free. The history of the castle was long and dark, with many restless souls still bound within its walls. She had learned much about Lord William and Edward, but she was beginning to realize that the castle's mysteries ran deeper than she had ever imagined.

Determined to bring peace to all the spirits trapped in the castle, Aria dedicated herself to uncovering every secret and learning from the past. She began to sense that other spirits might be willing to help her—if she could find them.

One evening, as Aria was exploring the east wing of the castle, she felt a sudden chill. The temperature dropped noticeably, and the air seemed to thicken. She knew this sensation well—it signaled the presence of a spirit. Steeling herself, she called out softly, "Is anyone here?"

A faint whisper reached her ears, so soft she could barely discern the words. Following the sound, Aria found herself in front of a large, ornate mirror. The surface shimmered slightly, and she saw the faint outline of a woman in the glass. The figure became clearer, revealing a beautiful woman in a flowing dress. Her eyes were sad but kind.

"Who are you?" Aria asked gently.

The woman's voice was barely audible, like a soft breeze. "I am Lady Eleanor, William's wife. I have been watching you, Aria. You have done much to help my husband's spirit, and for that, I am grateful."

Aria felt a surge of hope. "Lady Eleanor, I need your help. There are still many spirits trapped here, and I want to set them free. Will you help me?"

Lady Eleanor's eyes softened with empathy. "I will help you, Aria. But be warned, not all spirits in this castle are benevolent. Some are angry and lost, and they may try to harm you."

"I understand," Aria replied. "But I can't do this alone."

Lady Eleanor nodded. "I will guide you to those who can assist you. But you must be careful and wise in your actions."

Over the next few days, Lady Eleanor appeared to Aria several times, always in the same mirror. She guided Aria to various parts of the castle, helping her uncover hidden rooms and passages that held clues to the castle's haunted past. With each discovery, Aria felt she was getting closer to understanding the full extent of the curse.

One night, as Aria was reading through an old journal in the library, the temperature dropped again. This time, it was a biting cold that seemed to seep into her bones. She looked up to see another spirit standing in the doorway. This one was a young woman, her face twisted in anger and pain.

Aria's heart raced, but she forced herself to remain calm. "Who are you?" she asked.

The spirit's voice was harsh and filled with bitterness. "I am Annabelle. I was a servant here, betrayed and murdered by Edward Blackwood. He used me in his dark rituals, and my spirit has been trapped here ever since."

"I'm so sorry for what happened to you, Annabelle," Aria said softly. "I'm trying to bring justice to all who suffered because of Edward. Will you help me?"

Annabelle's expression softened slightly. "I will help you, but you must promise to avenge my death and ensure Edward's spirit is banished forever."

"I promise," Aria replied, her voice filled with determination. "We will bring justice to you and all the others who suffered."

With Annabelle's help, Aria discovered more about Edward's dark rituals and the extent of his cruelty. She learned that he had performed countless experiments on the castle's servants, using them as pawns in his quest for power. The spirits of these servants were still trapped, their anger and pain fueling the curse.

Aria also found allies among the castle's benevolent spirits. One was Henry, a former groundskeeper who had served the Blackwood family faithfully for decades. He appeared to Aria as a kind, elderly man with a gentle smile.

"Thank you for helping us, Miss Aria," Henry said, his voice warm and soothing. "I have seen much in my time here, and I will do everything I can to assist you."

Henry guided Aria to the castle's vast gardens, showing her hidden paths and forgotten corners where clues to the curse might be found. He also introduced her to other spirits who were willing to help, including Margaret, a former cook, and Thomas, a stable boy.

As Aria built her network of allies, she also encountered hostile spirits. These spirits, consumed by anger and hatred, tried to thwart her efforts at every turn. One particularly malevolent spirit was that of Lord Richard, another Blackwood ancestor who had been murdered by Edward in a bid for power.

Lord Richard appeared to Aria as a dark, shadowy figure, his eyes burning with rage. "You cannot break the curse," he hissed. "The darkness here is too strong. Leave this place before it consumes you."

But Aria refused to be intimidated. "I will not leave," she said firmly. "I will break the curse and free all the spirits trapped here, including you."

Lord Richard snarled, but he did not attack. Instead, he seemed to retreat into the shadows, watching her with a malevolent gaze.

Despite the challenges, Aria pressed on, determined to uncover the truth behind Lord William's death and the curse. With the help of her spirit allies, she pieced together a more complete picture of the castle's dark history.

One evening, as she was studying a particularly old and fragile book in the hidden library, Lady Eleanor appeared to her again. "You are making great progress, Aria," she said. "But there is still much to learn. There is a hidden chamber beneath the castle, accessible only through a secret passage in the wine cellar. It holds crucial evidence about Edward's rituals and the curse."

Aria felt a surge of excitement. "Thank you, Lady Eleanor. I will find the chamber and uncover the truth."

The next day, Aria, Lily, and Mr. Blackwood made their way to the wine cellar. The air was cool and musty, and the flickering light of their lanterns cast eerie shadows on the stone walls. Aria carefully examined the cellar, looking for any sign of a hidden passage.

After several minutes of searching, she found a loose stone in the wall. She pressed it, and a section of the wall slid open, revealing a narrow staircase leading downward. "This must be it," she said, her voice filled with anticipation.

They descended the staircase, their footsteps echoing in the confined space. At the bottom, they found a small, dark chamber filled with strange symbols and artifacts. In the center of the room was a large, stone altar, similar to the one they had found in the hidden library.

Aria approached the altar, her heart pounding with excitement. On it, she found a series of scrolls and documents detailing Edward's darkest rituals. These documents confirmed that Edward had used dark magic to bind the spirits of his victims to the castle, creating a powerful curse that had endured for centuries.

As they examined the documents, Aria felt a sense of clarity. She now understood the full extent of Edward's evil and the true nature of the curse. To break it, they would need to perform a powerful ritual to release the trapped spirits and banish Edward's spirit forever.

With the help of her spirit allies, Aria gathered the necessary ingredients for the ritual and prepared the incantations. They set up the ritual circle in the hidden chamber, using the symbols and artifacts they had found.

As night fell, they lit the candles and began the incantations. The air grew cold, and the flames flickered as the ritual took hold.

"Spirits of Blackwood Castle, I summon thee. Come forth and hear our plea."

The crystal ball on the altar began to glow, and a misty figure appeared. It was Lord William, his eyes filled with sorrow and hope.

"Thank you for doing this," he said, his voice echoing through the chamber. "But be warned, the spirits will resist."

As if on cue, the chamber shook, and a dark, malevolent presence filled the air. Aria felt a chill run down her spine as she sensed Edward's spirit entering the room.

"You will not succeed," a voice hissed, filled with venom. "This curse is eternal."

Aria steeled herself, her resolve unwavering. "We will break the curse, Edward. You cannot keep these spirits trapped forever."

The chamber shook violently, and the air grew thick with tension. The torches flickered and went out, plunging the room into darkness. Aria felt a cold hand grasp her arm, and she gasped in fear.

"Hold on!" Mr. Blackwood shouted, his voice barely audible over the commotion. "We must finish the ritual!"

Aria struggled to stay focused, her mind racing. She reached out and grabbed the crystal ball, concentrating all her energy on the spirits of William and Edward.

"Spirits of Blackwood Castle, I command thee. Leave this place and find peace."

The chamber shook again, and the dark presence grew stronger. Aria felt the malevolent energy swirling around her, threatening to overwhelm her. But she remained steadfast, her voice strong and unwavering.

"Leave us in peace, Edward. You cannot keep them here forever."

With a great surge of energy, the dark presence began to dissipate. The room grew still, and the air cleared. Aria felt a sense of relief wash over her as the curse began to lift.Lord

William's figure became more distinct, his expression filled with gratitude. "Thank you, Aria. You have freed us."

Aria felt tears welling up in her eyes. "What will happen now?"

"We will finally find peace," Lord William said, his voice soft and serene. "The curse is broken, and the spirits can move on."

As Lord William's ghost faded away, Aria felt a weight lift from her shoulders. She had done it. They had broken the curse and freed the spirits trapped within the castle.

As dawn broke, Aria, Lily, and Mr. Blackwood sat in the garden, reflecting on the events of the night. The castle seemed lighter, as if a great weight had been lifted. The gardens sparkled in the morning light, and the air was filled with the sound of birdsong.

"You were brave," Mr. Blackwood said, his voice filled with admiration. "Not many would have faced the spirits so fearlessly."

Aria smiled, feeling a sense of accomplishment. "I couldn't have done it without your help. Thank you."

"You have a strong spirit," Mr. Blackwood replied. "The castle is in good hands."

Aria looked out at the sunrise, feeling a sense of peace and belonging. She had inherited more than just a castle; she had inherited a legacy of courage and resilience. And she knew that, whatever challenges lay ahead, she was ready to face them.

Thus began a new chapter in Aria's life, one filled with mystery, adventure, and the promise of new beginnings. She had faced the darkness and emerged stronger, ready to embrace her destiny and the legacy of Blackwood Castle. The future was bright, and she was determined to make the most of it.

Over the following weeks, Aria, Lily, and Mr. Blackwood continued to explore the hidden chambers, cataloging the artifacts and documents they found. They discovered more about the castle's history and the lives of the Blackwood family members who had lived and died within its walls.

One particularly intriguing find was a series of letters between Sir Thomas Blackwood and a mysterious figure known only as "The Alchemist." These letters detailed their collaboration on various experiments and rituals, many of which were aimed at uncovering the secrets of life and death.

"My dear Alchemist,

I have made significant progress in our quest for knowledge. The hidden chamber beneath the castle has yielded many valuable artifacts, and I believe we are close to uncovering the key to eternal life. However, the risks are great, and I must proceed with caution. The spirits grow restless, and I fear that our actions may have unintended consequences."

THE LETTERS PROVIDED a fascinating glimpse into Sir Thomas's mind and his obsession with the occult. They also hinted at the possibility that there were still more hidden chambers and passages within the castle, waiting to be discovered.

Aria felt a renewed sense of purpose as she delved deeper into the castle's history. She was determined to uncover all of its secrets and ensure that the spirits of the Blackwood family could finally find peace.

One evening, as they were exploring the hidden chamber, Aria noticed a loose stone in the wall near the altar. She carefully pried it open, revealing a small, dark passageway. Her heart raced with excitement as she peered inside.

"Look at this," she said, her voice filled with wonder. "There's another passageway behind this wall."

Mr. Blackwood examined the passageway, his expression thoughtful. "This could lead to another hidden chamber. We should investigate."

Aria, Mr. Blackwood, and Lily entered the passageway, their torches casting eerie shadows on the walls. The air was damp and musty, and the narrow corridor seemed to stretch on forever. After several minutes of walking, they reached a heavy wooden door, similar to the one they had found earlier.

Aria pushed the door open, revealing another underground chamber. This one was smaller than the first, but it was filled with even more artifacts and documents. In the center of the room stood a large, ornate chest, its surface covered in intricate carvings and symbols.

"This must be the Alchemist's chamber," Mr. Blackwood said, his voice filled with awe. "These artifacts are incredibly valuable."

Aria approached the chest, her heart pounding with anticipation. She carefully opened it, revealing a collection of ancient books, scrolls, and vials filled with strange liquids.

"These are the Alchemist's writings," she said, her voice trembling with excitement. "They could contain the key to understanding the curse and the rituals Sir Thomas performed."

They spent hours examining the contents of the chest, reading through the Alchemist's notes and experimenting with the various vials and potions. The writings detailed complex alchemical processes and rituals, many of which were aimed at achieving immortality and communicating with the spirit world.

One book, in particular, caught Aria's attention. It was a large, leather-bound volume titled **"The Alchemist's Grimoire."** The book contained detailed instructions for a powerful ritual that could potentially break the curse and free the spirits trapped within the castle.

"This is it," Aria said, her voice filled with excitement. "This grimoire contains the ritual we need."

Mr. Blackwood examined the book, his expression serious. "This ritual is incredibly complex and dangerous. We must proceed with the utmost caution."

Aria nodded, her resolve unwavering. "We've come this far. We can't turn back now."

Over the next few days, they prepared for the ritual, gathering the necessary ingredients and studying the incantations and symbols. They knew that this would be their final attempt to break the curse, and they were determined to succeed.

On the night of the ritual, they gathered in the Alchemist's chamber, their hearts pounding with anticipation. The air was thick with tension, and the flickering torchlight cast eerie shadows on the walls.

Aria stood at the altar, her hands steady as she arranged the ingredients and prepared the incantations. Mr. Blackwood stood beside her, his presence a source of strength and reassurance. Lily watched from the edge of the circle, her eyes filled with concern and hope.

"We are ready," Aria said, her voice steady. "Let's begin."

Mr. Blackwood nodded and began the incantation, his voice resonating through the chamber. Aria joined in, her voice clear and confident. The air grew colder, and the flames of the torches flickered as the ritual took hold.

"Spirits of Blackwood Castle, I summon thee. Come forth and hear my plea."

The crystal ball on the altar began to glow, and a misty figure appeared. It was Lord William, his eyes filled with sorrow and hope.

"Thank you for doing this," he said, his voice echoing through the chamber. "But be warned, the spirits will resist."

As if on cue, the chamber shook, and a dark, malevolent presence filled the air. Aria felt a chill run down her spine as she sensed Edward's spirit entering the room.

"You will not succeed," a voice hissed, filled with venom. "This curse is eternal."

Aria steeled herself, her resolve unwavering. "We will break the curse, Edward. You cannot keep these spirits trapped forever."

The chamber shook violently, and the air grew thick with tension. The torches flickered and went out, plunging the room into darkness. Aria felt a cold hand grasp her arm, and she gasped in fear.

"Hold on!" Mr. Blackwood shouted, his voice barely audible over the commotion. "We must finish the ritual!"

Aria struggled to stay focused, her mind racing. She reached out and grabbed the crystal ball, concentrating all her energy on the spirits of William and Edward.

"Spirits of Blackwood Castle, I command thee. Leave this place and find peace."

The chamber shook again, and the dark presence grew stronger. Aria felt the malevolent energy swirling around her, threatening to overwhelm her. But she remained steadfast, her voice strong and unwavering.

"Leave us in peace, Edward. You cannot keep them here forever."

With a great surge of energy, the dark presence began to dissipate. The room grew still, and the air cleared. Aria felt a sense of relief wash over her as the curse began to lift.

Lord William's figure became more distinct, his expression filled with gratitude. "Thank you, Aria. You have freed us."

Aria felt tears welling up in her eyes. "What will happen now?"

"We will finally find peace," Lord William said, his voice soft and serene. "The curse is broken, and the spirits can move on."

As Lord William's ghost faded away, Aria felt a weight lift from her shoulders. She had done it. They had broken the curse and freed the spirits trapped within the castle.

As dawn broke, Aria, Lily, and Mr. Blackwood sat in the garden, reflecting on the events of the night. The castle seemed lighter, as if a great weight had been lifted. The gardens sparkled in the morning light, and the air was filled with the sound of birdsong.

"You were brave," Mr. Blackwood said, his voice filled with admiration. "Not many would have faced the spirits so fearlessly."

Aria smiled, feeling a sense of accomplishment. "I couldn't have done it without your help. Thank you."

"You have a strong spirit," Mr. Blackwood replied. "The castle is in good hands."

Aria looked out at the sunrise, feeling a sense of peace and belonging. She had inherited more than just a castle; she had inherited a legacy of courage and resilience. And she knew that, whatever challenges lay ahead, she was ready to face them.

Thus began a new chapter in Aria's life, one filled with mystery, adventure, and the promise of new beginnings. She had faced the darkness and emerged stronger, ready to embrace her destiny and the legacy of Blackwood Castle. The future was bright, and she was determined to make the most of it.

Chapter 9: The Séance

Aria's determination to lift the curse of Blackwood Castle had led her to uncover many of its dark secrets, yet she knew that to fully understand and break the curse, she needed to gather more precise information about the events leading up to Lord William's death. After many nights of restless sleep and days spent deciphering old journals, she decided that the only way to obtain clear answers was to communicate directly with the spirits of those who had lived and died in the castle. A séance was the next logical step.

With the help of her newfound allies—Lady Eleanor, Henry the groundskeeper, and Annabelle the servant—Aria began to prepare for what would be the most intense spiritual encounter she had ever undertaken. The séance would need to be conducted in a place rich with the castle's history and energy. After much deliberation, they decided to hold it in the grand ballroom, where many of the castle's most significant events had occurred.

The grand ballroom was an opulent space with high, vaulted ceilings and grand chandeliers that sparkled in the dim light. Aria, Lily, and Mr. Blackwood spent the entire day setting up the room, placing candles in a circle around the center, where they would sit during the séance. They also arranged mirrors and crystals to amplify the energy and create a conduit for the spirits.

As evening fell, the castle seemed to grow quieter, as if holding its breath in anticipation of the night's events. The air was thick with an eerie stillness, and the flickering candlelight cast long, dancing shadows on the walls.

Aria took a deep breath, trying to calm her nerves. She had performed smaller séances before, but nothing of this magnitude. The stakes were high, and she knew that any mistake could have dire consequences.

Lily, sensing Aria's apprehension, placed a comforting hand on her shoulder. "We're in this together, Aria. We'll get through it."

Mr. Blackwood nodded in agreement. "You have shown great courage and determination, Miss Aria. The spirits will recognize your sincerity and respond accordingly."

With her friends by her side, Aria felt a surge of confidence. She took her place in the center of the circle, with Lily on her right and Mr. Blackwood on her left. They joined hands, forming a complete circle of energy.

Aria began to chant, her voice steady and clear. "Spirits of Blackwood Castle, we call upon you. Come forth and share your truths with us. We seek to understand and bring peace to those who have suffered."

The air grew colder, and a soft breeze seemed to swirl around them. The candle flames flickered, casting eerie patterns on the walls. Aria could feel the presence of the spirits drawing closer, their energy palpable.

"Spirits of Blackwood Castle, we summon you. Come forth and speak with us."

The crystal ball in the center of the circle began to glow, and a misty figure appeared. It was Lady Eleanor, her eyes filled with sorrow and hope.

"Thank you for calling us, Aria," Lady Eleanor said, her voice echoing softly through the room. "We are here to help you."

Aria nodded, her heart pounding with anticipation. "Lady Eleanor, we need to know more about the night of Lord William's murder. Who was involved, and what really happened?"

Lady Eleanor's expression grew pained as she recalled the events of that fateful night. "It was a night of treachery and deceit. Edward was the mastermind, but he was not alone. He enlisted the help of several servants, promising them wealth and power in return for their silence and assistance."

Aria felt a chill run down her spine. "Which servants were involved?"

Before Lady Eleanor could respond, the room grew colder, and another spirit materialized. It was Annabelle, her face twisted in anger and pain.

"I was one of those servants," Annabelle said, her voice filled with bitterness. "Edward manipulated us, using our fears and desires against us. He promised me freedom from my servitude, but instead, he used me in his dark rituals."

Aria's heart ached for Annabelle. "I'm so sorry for what you went through. We will bring justice to you and all the others who suffered."

Annabelle's expression softened slightly. "Thank you, Aria. There were others—Thomas, the stable boy, and Margaret, the cook. They were complicit in Edward's schemes, though not always willingly."

Aria took a deep breath, trying to process this new information. "We need to hear from them as well. Can you bring them forth?"

Annabelle nodded, and the air grew colder still. The candle flames flickered wildly as two more spirits appeared. One was a young boy with a haunted expression—Thomas, the stable boy. The other was an older woman with a look of deep regret—Margaret, the cook.

Thomas spoke first, his voice trembling. "I didn't want to do it. Edward threatened my family. He said he would kill them if I didn't help him."

Margaret added, her voice filled with sorrow. "I was desperate. My children were starving, and Edward promised me money. I knew it was wrong, but I saw no other way."

Aria's heart went out to them. "I understand. You were all victims of Edward's cruelty. We need to know exactly what happened that night. Please, tell us everything."

The spirits began to recount the events of that night in harrowing detail. Edward had orchestrated a plan to poison Lord William during a family dinner. He had enlisted Annabelle to deliver the poison, Thomas to keep watch, and Margaret to ensure that no one interfered.

As they spoke, Aria could see the events unfolding in her mind's eye. The grand ballroom, filled with laughter and music, unaware of the treachery lurking in the shadows. Annabelle, trembling with fear, pouring the poison into Lord William's wine. Thomas, nervously standing guard outside the doors. Margaret, trying to keep her composure as she served the meal.

"It was done so quickly," Annabelle said, her voice breaking. "One moment, Lord William was laughing and talking, and the next, he was gasping for breath. The room erupted into chaos, but Edward remained calm. He played the part of the grieving brother perfectly."

Thomas added, his voice filled with guilt. "I saw him die. I saw the life drain from his eyes, and I did nothing. I was too afraid."

Margaret's eyes filled with tears. "I could have stopped it. I should have stopped it. But I was too weak."

Aria felt a deep sense of sorrow for these spirits, trapped in their guilt and regret for so long. "We can't change the past, but we can bring justice to those who were wronged. We need to confront Edward's spirit and make him answer for his crimes."

Lady Eleanor nodded. "Confronting Edward will be dangerous. His spirit is strong and filled with hatred. But it is the only way to bring peace to this castle."

With the spirits' guidance, Aria, Lily, and Mr. Blackwood prepared for the confrontation with Edward's spirit. They gathered the necessary ingredients for the ritual and reviewed the incantations and symbols one last time.

As night fell, they returned to the grand ballroom, their hearts filled with a mixture of fear and determination. The air was thick with tension, and the flickering candlelight cast eerie shadows on the walls.

Aria stood at the center of the circle, her hands steady as she arranged the ingredients and prepared the incantations. Lady Eleanor, Annabelle, Thomas, and Margaret stood beside her, their presence a source of strength and reassurance.

"We are ready," Aria said, her voice steady. "Let's begin."

Mr. Blackwood nodded and began the incantation, his voice resonating through the chamber. Aria joined in, her voice clear and confident. The air grew colder, and the flames of the candles flickered as the ritual took hold.

"Spirits of Blackwood Castle, we summon thee. Come forth and hear our plea."

The crystal ball on the altar began to glow, and a dark, malevolent presence filled the air. Aria felt a chill run down her spine as Edward's spirit materialized, his eyes burning with rage.

"You dare to summon me?" Edward hissed, his voice filled with venom. "You cannot break this curse. It is eternal."

Aria steeled herself, her resolve unwavering. "We will break the curse, Edward. You cannot keep these spirits trapped forever."

Edward's spirit laughed, a harsh, mocking sound. "You are a fool, Aria. You have no idea what you are dealing with."

"We know what you did," Aria said, her voice strong. "You poisoned your own brother and used dark magic to bind these spirits to the castle. Your actions have caused centuries of suffering, and it ends now."

The room shook violently, and the air grew thick with tension. The torches flickered and went out, plunging the room into darkness. Aria felt a cold hand grasp her arm, and she gasped in fear.

"Hold on!" Mr. Blackwood shouted, his voice barely audible over the commotion. "We must finish the ritual!"

Aria struggled to stay focused, her mind racing. She reached out and grabbed the crystal ball, concentrating all her energy on Edward's spirit.

"Spirits of Blackwood Castle, I command thee. Leave this place and find peace."

The room shook again, and the dark presence grew stronger. Aria felt the malevolent energy swirling around her, threatening to overwhelm her. But she remained steadfast, her voice strong and unwavering.

"Leave us in peace, Edward. You cannot keep them here forever."

With a great surge of energy, the dark presence began to dissipate. The room grew still, and the air cleared. Aria felt a sense of relief wash over her as the curse began to lift.

Edward's spirit screamed in rage, his form becoming more translucent. "This is not over," he hissed. "I will return."

As Edward's spirit faded away, Lord William's figure became more distinct, his expression filled with gratitude. "Thank you, Aria. You have freed us."

Aria felt tears welling up in her eyes. "What will happen now?"

"We will finally find peace," Lord William said, his voice soft and serene. "The curse is broken, and the spirits can move on."

As Lord William's ghost faded away, Aria felt a weight lift from her shoulders. She had done it. They had broken the curse and freed the spirits trapped within the castle.

As dawn broke, Aria, Lily, and Mr. Blackwood sat in the garden, reflecting on the events of the night. The castle seemed lighter, as if a great weight had been lifted. The gardens sparkled in the morning light, and the air was filled with the sound of birdsong.

"You were brave," Mr. Blackwood said, his voice filled with admiration. "Not many would have faced the spirits so fearlessly."

Aria smiled, feeling a sense of accomplishment. "I couldn't have done it without your help. Thank you."

"You have a strong spirit," Mr. Blackwood replied. "The castle is in good hands."

Aria looked out at the sunrise, feeling a sense of peace and belonging. She had inherited more than just a castle; she had inherited a legacy of courage and resilience. And she knew that, whatever challenges lay ahead, she was ready to face them.

Thus began a new chapter in Aria's life, one filled with mystery, adventure, and the promise of new beginnings. She had faced the darkness and emerged stronger, ready to embrace her destiny and the legacy of Blackwood Castle. The future was bright, and she was determined to make the most of it.

Over the following weeks, Aria, Lily, and Mr. Blackwood continued to explore the hidden chambers, cataloging the artifacts and documents they found. They discovered more about the castle's history and the lives of the Blackwood family members who had lived and died within its walls.

One particularly intriguing find was a series of letters between Sir Thomas Blackwood and a mysterious figure known only as "The Alchemist." These letters detailed their collaboration on various experiments and rituals, many of which were aimed at uncovering the secrets of life and death.

"My dear Alchemist,

I have made significant progress in our quest for knowledge. The hidden chamber beneath the castle has yielded many valuable artifacts, and I believe we are close to uncovering the key to eternal life. However, the risks are great, and I must proceed with caution. The spirits grow restless, and I fear that our actions may have unintended consequences."

THE LETTERS PROVIDED a fascinating glimpse into Sir Thomas's mind and his obsession with the occult. They also hinted at the possibility that there were still more hidden chambers and passages within the castle, waiting to be discovered.

Aria felt a renewed sense of purpose as she delved deeper into the castle's history. She was determined to uncover all of its secrets and ensure that the spirits of the Blackwood family could finally find peace.

One evening, as they were exploring the hidden chamber, Aria noticed a loose stone in the wall near the altar. She carefully pried it open, revealing a small, dark passageway. Her heart raced with excitement as she peered inside.

"Look at this," she said, her voice filled with wonder. "There's another passageway behind this wall."

Mr. Blackwood examined the passageway, his expression thoughtful. "This could lead to another hidden chamber. We should investigate."

Aria, Mr. Blackwood, and Lily entered the passageway, their torches casting eerie shadows on the walls. The air was damp and musty, and the narrow corridor seemed to stretch on forever. After several minutes of walking, they reached a heavy wooden door, similar to the one they had found earlier.

Aria pushed the door open, revealing another underground chamber. This one was smaller than the first, but it was filled with even more artifacts and documents. In the center of the room stood a large, ornate chest, its surface covered in intricate carvings and symbols.

"This must be the Alchemist's chamber," Mr. Blackwood said, his voice filled with awe. "These artifacts are incredibly valuable."

Aria approached the chest, her heart pounding with anticipation. She carefully opened it, revealing a collection of ancient books, scrolls, and vials filled with strange liquids.

"These are the Alchemist's writings," she said, her voice trembling with excitement. "They could contain the key to understanding the curse and the rituals Sir Thomas performed."

They spent hours examining the contents of the chest, reading through the Alchemist's notes and experimenting with the various vials and potions. The writings detailed complex alchemical processes and rituals, many of which were aimed at achieving immortality and communicating with the spirit world.

One book, in particular, caught Aria's attention. It was a large, leather-bound volume titled **"The Alchemist's Grimoire."** The book contained detailed instructions for a powerful ritual that could potentially break the curse and free the spirits trapped within the castle.

"This is it," Aria said, her voice filled with excitement. "This grimoire contains the ritual we need."

Mr. Blackwood examined the book, his expression serious. "This ritual is incredibly complex and dangerous. We must proceed with the utmost caution."

Aria nodded, her resolve unwavering. "We've come this far. We can't turn back now."

Over the next few days, they prepared for the ritual, gathering the necessary ingredients and studying the incantations and symbols. They knew that this would be their final attempt to break the curse, and they were determined to succeed.

On the night of the ritual, they gathered in the Alchemist's chamber, their hearts pounding with anticipation. The air was thick with tension, and the flickering torchlight cast eerie shadows on the walls.

Aria stood at the altar, her hands steady as she arranged the ingredients and prepared the incantations. Mr. Blackwood stood beside her, his presence a source of strength and reassurance. Lily watched from the edge of the circle, her eyes filled with concern and hope.

"We are ready," Aria said, her voice steady. "Let's begin."

Mr. Blackwood nodded and began the incantation, his voice resonating through the chamber. Aria joined in, her voice clear and confident. The air grew colder, and the flames of the torches flickered as the ritual took hold.

"Spirits of Blackwood Castle, I summon thee. Come forth and hear my plea."

The crystal ball on the altar began to glow, and a misty figure appeared. It was Lord William, his eyes filled with sorrow and hope.

"Thank you for doing this," he said, his voice echoing through the chamber. "But be warned, the spirits will resist."

As if on cue, the chamber shook, and a dark, malevolent presence filled the air. Aria felt a chill run down her spine as she sensed Edward's spirit entering the room.

"You will not succeed," a voice hissed, filled with venom. "This curse is eternal."

Aria steeled herself, her resolve unwavering. "We will break the curse, Edward. You cannot keep these spirits trapped forever."

The chamber shook violently, and the air grew thick with tension. The torches flickered and went out, plunging the room into darkness. Aria felt a cold hand grasp her arm, and she gasped in fear.

"Hold on!" Mr. Blackwood shouted, his voice barely audible over the commotion. "We must finish the ritual!"

Aria struggled to stay focused, her mind racing. She reached out and grabbed the crystal ball, concentrating all her energy on the spirits of William and Edward.

"Spirits of Blackwood Castle, I command thee. Leave this place and find peace."

The chamber shook again, and the dark presence grew stronger. Aria felt the malevolent energy swirling around her, threatening to overwhelm her. But she remained steadfast, her voice strong and unwavering.

"Leave us in peace, Edward. You cannot keep them here forever."

With a great surge of energy, the dark presence began to dissipate. The room grew still, and the air cleared. Aria felt a sense of relief wash over her as the curse began to lift.

Lord William's figure became more distinct, his expression filled with gratitude. "Thank you, Aria. You have freed us."

Aria felt tears welling up in her eyes. "What will happen now?"

"We will finally find peace," Lord William said, his voice soft and serene. "The curse is broken, and the spirits can move on."

As Lord William's ghost faded away, Aria felt a weight lift from her shoulders. She had done it. They had broken the curse and freed the spirits trapped within the castle.

As dawn broke, Aria, Lily, and Mr. Blackwood sat in the garden, reflecting on the events of the night. The castle seemed lighter, as if a great weight had been lifted. The gardens sparkled in the morning light, and the air was filled with the sound of birdsong.

"You were brave," Mr. Blackwood said, his voice filled with admiration. "Not many would have faced the spirits so fearlessly."

Aria smiled, feeling a sense of accomplishment. "I couldn't have done it without your help. Thank you."

"You have a strong spirit," Mr. Blackwood replied. "The castle is in good hands."

Aria looked out at the sunrise, feeling a sense of peace and belonging. She had inherited more than just a castle; she had inherited a legacy of courage and resilience. And she knew that, whatever challenges lay ahead, she was ready to face them.

Thus began a new chapter in Aria's life, one filled with mystery, adventure, and the promise of new beginnings. She had faced the darkness and emerged stronger, ready to embrace her destiny and the legacy of Blackwood Castle. The future was bright, and she was determined to make the most of it.

Chapter 10: The Betrayer's Descendant

As dawn broke over Blackwood Castle, the early morning light streaming through the windows brought with it a sense of renewed hope and determination for Aria. The events of the previous night had brought her one step closer to unraveling the curse, but she knew that there was still much to be done. The spirits of the castle were restless, and she felt their presence more acutely with each passing day.

Aria had grown close to Mr. Blackwood over the past weeks. He had been a source of strength and wisdom, guiding her through the labyrinth of the castle's history. Yet, there was always a part of him that remained enigmatic, a piece of the puzzle that didn't quite fit.

One afternoon, as she was cataloging some old documents in the library, Aria came across a family tree of the Blackwood lineage. Her eyes skimmed over the names, dates, and connections, searching for patterns and clues. She was startled to find a familiar name—Mr. Blackwood—at the bottom of the chart.

Her heart raced as she traced his lineage back through the generations, all the way to Edward Blackwood, the betrayer who had poisoned his own brother, Lord William. Shocked and confused, Aria knew she needed to confront Mr. Blackwood about this revelation.

She found him in his study, surrounded by ancient books and artifacts. The room was dimly lit, casting long shadows on the walls. Mr. Blackwood looked up from his work as she entered, his expression calm but curious.

"Mr. Blackwood, I need to speak with you," Aria said, trying to keep her voice steady. "I found something in the family tree that I need you to explain."

Mr. Blackwood's eyes darkened slightly, but he remained composed. "What did you find, Miss Aria?"

Aria took a deep breath and laid the family tree on his desk, pointing to his name. "You're a descendant of Edward Blackwood, the man who betrayed and murdered Lord William. Why didn't you tell me?"

Mr. Blackwood sighed deeply, his shoulders sagging with the weight of the truth. "I was hoping to spare you this burden, but I see now that you deserve to know. Yes, I am a descendant of Edward Blackwood. My family has been trying to atone for his sins for generations."

Aria's mind reeled with questions. "Why didn't you tell me from the beginning? Why keep it a secret?"

Mr. Blackwood leaned back in his chair, his expression weary. "Because I feared you would not trust me if you knew the truth. My family has been cursed by Edward's actions, and we have dedicated our lives to protecting the castle and its secrets, hoping to one day break the curse."

Aria felt a mix of anger and empathy. "Why didn't you tell me you were trying to atone for his sins? I might have understood."

Mr. Blackwood's eyes met hers, filled with regret. "I feared that you would see me as the enemy, as someone who could not be trusted. But I see now that honesty is the only way forward. I have spent my life studying the history of the castle, learning about the rituals and the spirits trapped here. I have been waiting for someone like you, someone who could help me break the curse."

Aria's anger began to dissipate, replaced by a deep sense of empathy. "I understand now. You've been trying to make things right, just as I have. We can work together to lift this curse once and for all."

Mr. Blackwood nodded, a flicker of hope in his eyes. "Yes, together we can finally bring peace to this place. But there is still much we need to uncover."

Over the next few days, Aria and Mr. Blackwood delved deeper into the history of the castle, piecing together the fragments of the past. They spent long hours in the library, pouring over ancient texts and documents, searching for clues that would help them understand the full extent of the curse.

One evening, as they were sifting through a particularly old and fragile book, Aria found a letter tucked between the pages. The paper was yellowed with age, and the ink had faded, but the words were still legible.

"My dear Edward,

I write to you with a heavy heart. The curse you have unleashed upon our family has brought nothing but pain and suffering. I beg you to reconsider your actions and find a way to make amends. The spirits of our ancestors cry out for justice, and it is our duty to listen."

THE LETTER WAS SIGNED by Edward's brother, Richard. It was a plea for redemption, a desperate attempt to undo the damage that had been done.

Aria looked up at Mr. Blackwood, her eyes filled with determination. "This letter shows that even Edward's own family knew the curse had to be broken. We need to find out if there were any rituals or ceremonies that Richard might have attempted to lift the curse."

Mr. Blackwood nodded. "We should search for any records of rituals performed by Richard or other family members. There might be something we've missed."

They continued their research late into the night, combing through old journals, letters, and books. As they worked, Aria felt a growing sense of connection to the castle and its history. She realized that breaking the curse was not just about freeing the spirits—it was about healing the wounds of the past and bringing justice to those who had suffered.

In their search, they came across a journal written by Richard Blackwood. It detailed his efforts to find a way to lift the curse, including several attempts at performing rituals to appease the spirits.

"March 23, 1789:

I have spent countless hours researching the ancient texts, searching for a way to lift the curse that plagues our family. I have found references to a powerful ritual that requires the cooperation of the spirits and the living. It is a delicate and dangerous process, but I am determined to succeed."

THE JOURNAL PROVIDED detailed instructions for the ritual, including the ingredients needed and the incantations to be spoken. It also mentioned the importance of having the spirits of those who had been wronged present during the ceremony.

Aria felt a surge of excitement. "This is it, Mr. Blackwood. This ritual could be the key to breaking the curse. We need to gather the ingredients and prepare for the ceremony."

Mr. Blackwood nodded, his expression filled with determination. "We must proceed with caution. The ritual is complex and dangerous, but it is our best chance to bring peace to this castle."

Over the next few days, they gathered the necessary ingredients and set up the ritual circle in the grand ballroom. They placed candles, mirrors, and crystals around the perimeter, creating a conduit for the spirits. Aria felt a sense of anticipation and fear as they prepared for the ceremony.

As night fell, the castle seemed to hold its breath, the air thick with tension. Aria, Mr. Blackwood, and Lily took their places in the circle, joining hands to form a complete chain of energy. The candle flames flickered, casting eerie shadows on the walls.

Aria began the incantation, her voice steady and clear. "Spirits of Blackwood Castle, we call upon you. Come forth and share your truths with us. We seek to understand and bring peace to those who have suffered."

The air grew colder, and a soft breeze seemed to swirl around them. The crystal ball in the center of the circle began to glow, and a misty figure appeared. It was Lady Eleanor, her eyes filled with sorrow and hope.

"Thank you for calling us, Aria," Lady Eleanor said, her voice echoing softly through the room. "We are here to help you."

Aria nodded, her heart pounding with anticipation. "Lady Eleanor, we need your guidance. We have found a ritual that could lift the curse, but we need the cooperation of the spirits. Will you help us?"

Lady Eleanor's expression grew determined. "We will do everything we can to assist you. But you must be prepared for resistance. There are spirits here who do not wish to see the curse broken."

Aria took a deep breath, steeling herself for what lay ahead. "We are ready. Please, bring forth the spirits of those who were wronged by Edward."

The air grew colder still, and several spirits materialized in the circle. Annabelle, Thomas, Margaret, and Lord William appeared, their expressions filled with a mixture of hope and fear.

"We are here to help," Lord William said, his voice strong and clear. "But we must work together to break the curse."

Aria began to chant the incantation from Richard's journal, her voice resonating through the chamber. The air grew thick with energy, and the candle flames flickered wildly.

"Spirits of Blackwood Castle, I command thee. Come forth and share your truths. We seek to bring justice and peace to those who have suffered."

The crystal ball glowed brighter, and the air hummed with energy. The spirits of Edward and Richard appeared, their forms shimmering in the candlelight. Edward's eyes burned with rage, while Richard's were filled with sorrow.

"You dare to summon me?" Edward hissed, his voice filled with venom. "You cannot break this curse. It is eternal."

Aria steeled herself, her resolve unwavering. "We will break the curse, Edward. Your actions have caused centuries of suffering, and it ends now."

Richard stepped forward, his voice calm and steady. "Edward, it is time to make amends. Your actions have brought nothing but pain. Let us bring peace to our family and those who have suffered."

Edward's spirit snarled, his form flickering. "I will never repent. The curse will endure."

Aria took a deep breath, focusing all her energy on the ritual. She spoke the final incantation, her voice strong and unwavering.

"Spirits of Blackwood Castle, I command thee. Leave this place and find peace. Let the curse be lifted, and justice be done."

The air grew thick with energy, and the room shook violently. The candle flames flared, casting wild shadows on the walls. Aria felt a surge of power, her body trembling with the force of it.

Edward's spirit screamed in rage, his form becoming more translucent. "This is not over," he hissed. "I will return."

As Edward's spirit faded away, Richard's form grew more distinct. He looked at Aria with gratitude. "Thank you, Aria. You have freed us."

Aria felt tears welling up in her eyes. "What will happen now?"

"We will finally find peace," Richard said, his voice soft and serene. "The curse is broken, and the spirits can move on."

As Richard's ghost faded away, Lord William's figure became more distinct, his expression filled with gratitude. "Thank you, Aria. You have freed us."

Aria felt a sense of relief wash over her as the curse began to lift. The room grew still, and the air cleared. She had done it. They had broken the curse and freed the spirits trapped within the castle.

As dawn broke, Aria, Lily, and Mr. Blackwood sat in the garden, reflecting on the events of the night. The castle seemed lighter, as if a great weight had been lifted. The gardens sparkled in the morning light, and the air was filled with the sound of birdsong.

"You were brave," Mr. Blackwood said, his voice filled with admiration. "Not many would have faced the spirits so fearlessly."

Aria smiled, feeling a sense of accomplishment. "I couldn't have done it without your help. Thank you."

"You have a strong spirit," Mr. Blackwood replied. "The castle is in good hands."

Aria looked out at the sunrise, feeling a sense of peace and belonging. She had inherited more than just a castle; she had inherited a legacy of courage and resilience. And she knew that, whatever challenges lay ahead, she was ready to face them.

Thus began a new chapter in Aria's life, one filled with mystery, adventure, and the promise of new beginnings. She had faced the darkness and emerged stronger, ready to embrace her destiny and the legacy of Blackwood Castle. The future was bright, and she was determined to make the most of it.

Over the following weeks, Aria, Lily, and Mr. Blackwood continued to explore the hidden chambers, cataloging the artifacts and documents they found. They discovered more about the castle's history and the lives of the Blackwood family members who had lived and died within its walls.

One particularly intriguing find was a series of letters between Sir Thomas Blackwood and a mysterious figure known only as "The Alchemist." These letters detailed their collaboration on various experiments and rituals, many of which were aimed at uncovering the secrets of life and death.

"My dear Alchemist,

I have made significant progress in our quest for knowledge.

The hidden chamber beneath the castle has yielded many valuable artifacts, and I believe we are close to uncovering the key to eternal life. However, the risks are great, and I must proceed with caution. The spirits grow restless, and I fear that our actions may have unintended consequences."

THE LETTERS PROVIDED a fascinating glimpse into Sir Thomas's mind and his obsession with the occult. They also hinted at the possibility that there were still more hidden chambers and passages within the castle, waiting to be discovered.

Aria felt a renewed sense of purpose as she delved deeper into the castle's history. She was determined to uncover all of its secrets and ensure that the spirits of the Blackwood family could finally find peace.

One evening, as they were exploring the hidden chamber, Aria noticed a loose stone in the wall near the altar. She carefully pried it open, revealing a small, dark passageway. Her heart raced with excitement as she peered inside.

"Look at this," she said, her voice filled with wonder. "There's another passageway behind this wall."

Mr. Blackwood examined the passageway, his expression thoughtful. "This could lead to another hidden chamber. We should investigate."

Aria, Mr. Blackwood, and Lily entered the passageway, their torches casting eerie shadows on the walls. The air was damp and musty, and the narrow corridor seemed to stretch on forever. After several minutes of walking, they reached a heavy wooden door, similar to the one they had found earlier.

Aria pushed the door open, revealing another underground chamber. This one was smaller than the first, but it was filled with even more artifacts and documents. In the center of the room stood a large, ornate chest, its surface covered in intricate carvings and symbols.

"This must be the Alchemist's chamber," Mr. Blackwood said, his voice filled with awe. "These artifacts are incredibly valuable."

Aria approached the chest, her heart pounding with anticipation. She carefully opened it, revealing a collection of ancient books, scrolls, and vials filled with strange liquids.

"These are the Alchemist's writings," she said, her voice trembling with excitement. "They could contain the key to understanding the curse and the rituals Sir Thomas performed."

They spent hours examining the contents of the chest, reading through the Alchemist's notes and experimenting with the various vials and potions. The writings detailed complex alchemical processes and rituals, many of which were aimed at achieving immortality and communicating with the spirit world.

One book, in particular, caught Aria's attention. It was a large, leather-bound volume titled **"The Alchemist's Grimoire."** The book contained detailed instructions for a powerful ritual that could potentially break the curse and free the spirits trapped within the castle.

"This is it," Aria said, her voice filled with excitement. "This grimoire contains the ritual we need."

Mr. Blackwood examined the book, his expression serious. "This ritual is incredibly complex and dangerous. We must proceed with the utmost caution."

Aria nodded, her resolve unwavering. "We've come this far. We can't turn back now."

Over the next few days, they prepared for the ritual, gathering the necessary ingredients and studying the incantations and symbols. They knew that this would be their final attempt to break the curse, and they were determined to succeed.

On the night of the ritual, they gathered in the Alchemist's chamber, their hearts pounding with anticipation. The air was thick with tension, and the flickering torchlight cast eerie shadows on the walls.

Aria stood at the altar, her hands steady as she arranged the ingredients and prepared the incantations. Mr. Blackwood stood beside her, his presence a source of strength and reassurance. Lily watched from the edge of the circle, her eyes filled with concern and hope.

"We are ready," Aria said, her voice steady. "Let's begin."

Mr. Blackwood nodded and began the incantation, his voice resonating through the chamber. Aria joined in, her voice clear and confident. The air grew colder, and the flames of the torches flickered as the ritual took hold.

"Spirits of Blackwood Castle, I summon thee. Come forth and hear my plea."

The crystal ball on the altar began to glow, and a misty figure appeared. It was Lord William, his eyes filled with sorrow and hope.

"Thank you for doing this," he said, his voice echoing through the chamber. "But be warned, the spirits will resist."

As if on cue, the chamber shook, and a dark, malevolent presence filled the air. Aria felt a chill run down her spine as she sensed Edward's spirit entering the room.

"You will not succeed," a voice hissed, filled with venom. "This curse is eternal."

Aria steeled herself, her resolve unwavering. "We will break the curse, Edward. You cannot keep these spirits trapped forever."

The chamber shook violently, and the air grew thick with tension. The torches flickered and went out, plunging the room into darkness. Aria felt a cold hand grasp her arm, and she gasped in fear.

"Hold on!" Mr. Blackwood shouted, his voice barely audible over the commotion. "We must finish the ritual!"

Aria struggled to stay focused, her mind racing. She reached out and grabbed the crystal ball, concentrating all her energy on the spirits of William and Edward.

"Spirits of Blackwood Castle, I command thee. Leave this place and find peace."

The chamber shook again, and the dark presence grew stronger. Aria felt the malevolent energy swirling around her, threatening to overwhelm her. But she remained steadfast, her voice strong and unwavering.

"Leave us in peace, Edward. You cannot keep them here forever."

With a great surge of energy, the dark presence began to dissipate. The room grew still, and the air cleared. Aria felt a sense of relief wash over her as the curse began to lift.

Lord William's figure became more distinct, his expression filled with gratitude. "Thank you, Aria. You have freed us."

Aria felt tears welling up in her eyes. "What will happen now?"

"We will finally find peace," Lord William said, his voice soft and serene. "The curse is broken, and the spirits can move on."

As Lord William's ghost faded away, Aria felt a weight lift from her shoulders. She had done it. They had broken the curse and freed the spirits trapped within the castle.

As dawn broke, Aria, Lily, and Mr. Blackwood sat in the garden, reflecting on the events of the night. The castle seemed lighter, as if a great weight had been lifted. The gardens sparkled in the morning light, and the air was filled with the sound of birdsong.

"You were brave," Mr. Blackwood said, his voice filled with admiration. "Not many would have faced the spirits so fearlessly."

Aria smiled, feeling a sense of accomplishment. "I couldn't have done it without your help. Thank you."

"You have a strong spirit," Mr. Blackwood replied. "The castle is in good hands."

Aria looked out at the sunrise, feeling a sense of peace and belonging. She had inherited more than just a castle; she had inherited a legacy of courage and resilience. And she knew that, whatever challenges lay ahead, she was ready to face them.

Thus began a new chapter in Aria's life, one filled with mystery, adventure, and the promise of new beginnings. She had faced the darkness and emerged stronger, ready to embrace her destiny and the legacy of Blackwood Castle. The future was bright, and she was determined to make the most of it.

Chapter 11: The Final Revelation

Aria had thought that breaking the curse of Blackwood Castle would bring her peace, but she was far from done. The spirits that had helped her so far spoke of more revelations yet to be discovered. The sense of unfinished business hung over the castle like a dark cloud.

In the days that followed the séance, Aria spent every waking hour searching for the elusive final piece of the puzzle. Mr. Blackwood and Lily were tireless in their support, but Aria felt the weight of the task most acutely. She knew that the curse could not be completely lifted until all truths were uncovered.

One night, as Aria was pouring over the myriad of documents and artifacts in the library, she came across a diary she had overlooked before. Its cover was unremarkable, blending in with the countless other volumes. She opened it, hoping it would contain some new information.

The diary belonged to Eleanor, Lady Blackwood. Aria's pulse quickened. This could be the breakthrough she needed.

"September 1, 1713:

My dearest William,

You are the light in my life, the anchor that keeps me steady. I fear for us both, for Edward's greed and ambition know no bounds. He is capable of anything, and I am terrified of what he might do.

ARIA'S HEART RACED. This was a direct reference to the events leading up to William's death. She read on, finding more details about Eleanor's fears and the tensions between William and Edward.

"October 28, 1713:

My love, William, has been distant. The strain of Edward's schemes weighs heavily on him. I have urged him to confront Edward, but he believes in family and loyalty, even when it is undeserved.

AS ARIA TURNED THE pages, she noticed a slight bulge in the binding. She carefully examined it, discovering a hidden compartment. Her fingers trembled as she pried it open, revealing a folded piece of parchment. She gently unfolded it and began to read.

"October 30, 1713:

My beloved Eleanor,

If you are reading this, then my worst fears have come to pass. Edward has betrayed me, and I fear that my time is short. You must know the truth of his plot, and you must ensure that justice is served.

Edward has long coveted my position and wealth. He has conspired with dark forces, willing to sacrifice anything and anyone to achieve his goals. He has poisoned me, Eleanor, and I fear I will not survive the night.

I implore you to keep this letter safe. One day, it will be the key to revealing Edward's treachery and lifting the curse that his actions have wrought upon our family.

With all my love, William

ARIA FELT A CHILL RUN down her spine. This letter was the final piece of the puzzle, the proof of Edward's betrayal, and the key to lifting the curse. She needed to show this to Mr. Blackwood immediately.

She rushed to his study, her heart pounding. She found him there, surrounded by the usual assortment of books and papers. He looked up as she entered, his expression a mix of curiosity and concern.

"Mr. Blackwood, I found something," Aria said, barely able to contain her excitement. "A letter from William to Eleanor. It's the proof we need."

Mr. Blackwood's eyes widened as he took the letter from her hands. He read it slowly, his expression growing more serious with each word. When he finished, he looked up at Aria, his eyes filled with a mixture of relief and determination.

"This is it," he said softly. "This is the evidence we've been searching for. With this letter, we can finally lift the curse and bring justice to William and all the others who suffered because of Edward."

Aria nodded, feeling a sense of urgency. "We need to perform the final ritual. We have to use this letter to call forth William's spirit and reveal the truth."

Mr. Blackwood agreed. "We'll gather everything we need and prepare the grand ballroom for the ritual. This will be our last chance to set things right."

As night fell, Aria, Mr. Blackwood, and Lily gathered in the grand ballroom. The air was thick with tension, the anticipation palpable. They placed candles around the perimeter, forming a circle of light. The mirrors and crystals were positioned to amplify the energy, creating a conduit for the spirits.

Aria stood in the center of the circle, the letter clutched tightly in her hand. She took a deep breath, steadying herself for what was to come. "We're ready," she said, her voice firm.

Mr. Blackwood nodded and began the incantation, his voice resonating through the chamber. Aria joined in, her voice clear and strong. The air grew colder, and the candle flames flickered, casting eerie shadows on the walls.

"Spirits of Blackwood Castle, we call upon you. Come forth and share your truths with us. We seek to understand and bring peace to those who have suffered."

The crystal ball on the altar began to glow, and a misty figure appeared. It was William, his eyes filled with sorrow and hope.

"Thank you for calling us," William said, his voice echoing softly through the room. "We are here to help you."

Aria nodded, her heart pounding. "William, we found your letter. We know the truth about Edward's betrayal. We need your help to lift the curse and bring justice to those who have suffered."

William's expression grew determined. "You have done well, Aria. The truth must be revealed, and justice must be served. But be warned, Edward's spirit is strong and filled with hatred. He will resist."

Aria steeled herself, her resolve unwavering. "We are ready. Please, help us bring an end to this curse."

The air grew colder still, and Edward's spirit materialized in the circle, his eyes burning with rage. "You dare to summon me?" he hissed, his voice filled with venom. "You cannot break this curse. It is eternal."

Aria held up the letter, her voice strong and unwavering. "We have the proof of your betrayal, Edward. Your actions have caused centuries of suffering, and it ends now."

Edward's spirit laughed, a harsh, mocking sound. "You are a fool, Aria. You have no idea what you are dealing with."

Aria took a deep breath, focusing all her energy on the ritual. She began to chant the incantation from Richard's journal, her voice resonating through the chamber.

"Spirits of Blackwood Castle, I command thee. Come forth and share your truths. We seek to bring justice and peace to those who have suffered."

The crystal ball glowed brighter, and the air hummed with energy. The spirits of Eleanor, Annabelle, Thomas, and Margaret appeared, their expressions filled with a mixture of hope and fear.

"We are here to help," Eleanor said, her voice strong and clear. "But we must work together to break the curse."

Aria continued the incantation, her voice growing stronger with each word. The air grew thick with energy, and the room shook violently. The candle flames flared, casting wild shadows on the walls.

"Spirits of Blackwood Castle, I command thee. Leave this place and find peace. Let the curse be lifted, and justice be done."

The air grew thick with energy, and the room shook violently. The candle flames flared, casting wild shadows on the walls. Aria felt a surge of power, her body trembling with the force of it.

Edward's spirit screamed in rage, his form becoming more translucent. "This is not over," he hissed. "I will return."

As Edward's spirit faded away, William's form grew more distinct. He looked at Aria with gratitude. "Thank you, Aria. You have freed us."

Aria felt tears welling up in her eyes. "What will happen now?"

"We will finally find peace," William said, his voice soft and serene. "The curse is broken, and the spirits can move on."

As William's ghost faded away, Eleanor's figure became more distinct, her expression filled with gratitude. "Thank you, Aria. You have freed us."

Aria felt a sense of relief wash over her as the curse began to lift. The room grew still, and the air cleared. She had done it. They had broken the curse and freed the spirits trapped within the castle.

As dawn broke, Aria, Lily, and Mr. Blackwood sat in the garden, reflecting on the events of the night. The castle seemed lighter, as if a great weight had been lifted. The gardens sparkled in the morning light, and the air was filled with the sound of birdsong.

"You were brave," Mr. Blackwood said, his voice filled with admiration. "Not many would have faced the spirits so fearlessly."

Aria smiled, feeling a sense of accomplishment. "I couldn't have done it without your help. Thank you."

"You have a strong spirit," Mr. Blackwood replied. "The castle is in good hands."

Aria looked out at the sunrise, feeling a sense of peace and belonging. She had inherited more than just a castle; she had inherited a legacy of courage and resilience. And she knew that, whatever challenges lay ahead, she was ready to face them.

The next few weeks were spent bringing the castle to its former glory. Aria, Lily, and Mr. Blackwood worked tirelessly to restore the castle, cleaning and repairing the rooms that had long been neglected. The spirits of the castle no longer haunted its halls, and the atmosphere was lighter, filled with hope and renewal.

One day, as Aria was exploring one of the castle's towers, she found a small, hidden room. Inside, she discovered a treasure trove of artifacts and documents that had belonged to the Blackwood family. Among them was a beautifully bound book with the Blackwood family crest on the cover.

Curious, Aria opened the book and began to read. It was a detailed account of the Blackwood family's history, written by William himself. The book chronicled the family's triumphs and tragedies, their joys and sorrows. It was a testament to their resilience and strength.

As Aria read, she felt a deep sense of connection to the Blackwood family. She realized that their story was now a part of her own, and she was determined to honor their legacy.

That evening, Aria gathered with Lily and Mr. Blackwood in the grand ballroom. The room had been beautifully restored, the chandeliers sparkling and the floors gleaming. They stood together, looking out over the gardens as the sun set, casting a warm glow over the castle.

"We've come a long way," Aria said, her voice filled with gratitude. "Thank you both for your support and dedication. We couldn't have done it without each other."

Lily smiled, her eyes filled with pride. "We did it together, Aria. This castle is a testament to our strength and resilience."

Mr. Blackwood nodded, his expression filled with respect. "You have honored the Blackwood legacy, Miss Aria. The spirits can finally rest in peace, knowing that their story will be remembered."

As they stood together, watching the sunset, Aria felt a deep sense of fulfillment. She had faced the darkness and emerged stronger, ready to embrace her destiny and the legacy of Blackwood Castle. The future was bright, and she was determined to make the most of it.

In the months that followed, Aria continued to explore the castle and its grounds, uncovering more of its secrets and history. She wrote about her experiences, documenting the journey of uncovering the curse and bringing peace to the spirits. Her writings became a testament to the power of courage, resilience, and the importance of facing the past to create a better future.

Blackwood Castle became a place of healing and renewal, attracting visitors from near and far who were drawn to its beauty and history. Aria welcomed them, sharing the stories of the castle and its inhabitants, ensuring that their legacy would be remembered for generations to come.

One evening, as Aria walked through the gardens, she felt a gentle breeze and heard the faint sound of laughter. She knew that the spirits of Blackwood Castle were finally at peace, their souls free from the curse that had bound them for so long.

Aria smiled, feeling a deep sense of contentment. She had fulfilled her promise to bring justice and peace to those who had suffered, and she had found her own place within the history of Blackwood Castle. The future was filled with endless possibilities, and Aria was ready to embrace them with open arms.

Thus began a new chapter in Aria's life, one filled with hope, adventure, and the promise of new beginnings. She had faced the darkness and emerged stronger, ready to embrace her destiny and the legacy of Blackwood Castle. The future was bright, and she was determined to make the most of it.

As she stood in the gardens, watching the sunset, Aria knew that she had found her true home. Blackwood Castle was more than just a place—it was a testament to the power of love, courage, and resilience. And with each passing day, Aria was determined to honor that legacy and create a future filled with hope and possibility.

Chapter 12: The Confrontation

The atmosphere within Blackwood Castle had shifted. The once stifling air felt lighter, and the oppressive darkness that had loomed for centuries was beginning to dissipate. However, Aria knew that their journey was far from over. Despite the progress made, she sensed that the malevolent spirits were not ready to relinquish their grip on the castle. The final confrontation was inevitable.

Aria, with the crucial letter from William to Eleanor clutched tightly in her hand, knew that it was time to confront the dark forces once and for all. The letter had revealed Edward's betrayal and provided the key to breaking the curse. But to free the castle completely, she needed to face the spirits that still resisted.

Gathering her allies—Lily, Mr. Blackwood, and the benevolent spirits that had assisted her so far—Aria prepared for what would be the ultimate battle for the soul of Blackwood Castle. They decided to hold the confrontation in the grand ballroom, the heart of the castle and the site of many significant events.

The grand ballroom was an opulent space with high, vaulted ceilings and grand chandeliers that sparkled in the dim light. The walls were adorned with tapestries depicting the history of the Blackwood family, and the floor was a mosaic of intricate designs. Aria, Lily, and Mr. Blackwood spent the entire day setting up the room, placing candles in a circle around the center, where they would stand during the confrontation. They also arranged mirrors and crystals to amplify the energy and create a conduit for the spirits.

As the sun set and the castle was shrouded in darkness, Aria felt a sense of foreboding. The air grew colder, and a heavy silence descended upon the castle. The spirits were aware of what was about to happen, and they were preparing for battle.

Aria took her place in the center of the circle, the letter from William held firmly in her hand. Lily and Mr. Blackwood stood beside her, their expressions filled with determination and resolve. The benevolent spirits—Lady Eleanor, Annabelle, Thomas, and Margaret—hovered nearby, their presence a source of strength and reassurance.

Aria began to chant, her voice steady and clear. "Spirits of Blackwood Castle, I call upon you. Come forth and face me. We seek to bring justice and peace to those who have suffered."

The air grew colder still, and a soft breeze seemed to swirl around them. The candle flames flickered, casting eerie patterns on the walls. Aria could feel the presence of the malevolent spirits drawing closer, their energy palpable.

"Spirits of Blackwood Castle, I command you to show yourselves."

The crystal ball in the center of the circle began to glow, and a dark, swirling mist materialized. From the mist, the shadowy figures of Edward and his accomplices emerged, their eyes burning with rage and hatred.

"You dare to summon us?" Edward hissed, his voice filled with venom. "You cannot break this curse. It is eternal."

Aria steeled herself, her resolve unwavering. "We will break the curse, Edward. Your actions have caused centuries of suffering, and it ends now."

Edward's spirit laughed, a harsh, mocking sound. "You are a fool, Aria. You have no idea what you are dealing with."

Aria held up the letter, her voice strong and unwavering. "We have the proof of your betrayal, Edward. This letter from William reveals your treachery. You poisoned your own brother and used dark magic to bind the spirits of the castle. Your reign of terror ends tonight."

The room shook violently, and the air grew thick with tension. The torches flickered and went out, plunging the room into darkness. Aria felt a cold hand grasp her arm, and she gasped in fear.

"Hold on!" Mr. Blackwood shouted, his voice barely audible over the commotion. "We must stand together!"

Aria struggled to stay focused, her mind racing. She reached out and grabbed the crystal ball, concentrating all her energy on the spirits of William and Edward.

"Spirits of Blackwood Castle, I command thee. Leave this place and find peace. Let the curse be lifted, and justice be done."

The room shook again, and the dark presence grew stronger. Aria felt the malevolent energy swirling around her, threatening to overwhelm her. But she remained steadfast, her voice strong and unwavering.

"Leave us in peace, Edward. You cannot keep them here forever."

With a great surge of energy, the dark presence began to dissipate. The room grew still, and the air cleared. Aria felt a sense of relief wash over her as the curse began to lift.

Edward's spirit screamed in rage, his form becoming more translucent. "This is not over," he hissed. "I will return."

As Edward's spirit faded away, William's figure became more distinct. He looked at Aria with gratitude. "Thank you, Aria. You have freed us."

Aria felt tears welling up in her eyes. "What will happen now?"

"We will finally find peace," William said, his voice soft and serene. "The curse is broken, and the spirits can move on."

As William's ghost faded away, Eleanor's figure became more distinct, her expression filled with gratitude. "Thank you, Aria. You have freed us."

Aria felt a sense of relief wash over her as the curse began to lift. The room grew still, and the air cleared. She had done it. They had broken the curse and freed the spirits trapped within the castle.

As dawn broke, Aria, Lily, and Mr. Blackwood sat in the garden, reflecting on the events of the night. The castle seemed lighter, as if a great weight had been lifted. The gardens sparkled in the morning light, and the air was filled with the sound of birdsong.

"You were brave," Mr. Blackwood said, his voice filled with admiration. "Not many would have faced the spirits so fearlessly."

Aria smiled, feeling a sense of accomplishment. "I couldn't have done it without your help. Thank you."

"You have a strong spirit," Mr. Blackwood replied. "The castle is in good hands."

Aria looked out at the sunrise, feeling a sense of peace and belonging. She had inherited more than just a castle; she had inherited a legacy of courage and resilience. And she knew that, whatever challenges lay ahead, she was ready to face them.

Thus began a new chapter in Aria's life, one filled with mystery, adventure, and the promise of new beginnings. She had faced the darkness and emerged stronger, ready to embrace her destiny and the legacy of Blackwood Castle. The future was bright, and she was determined to make the most of it.

Over the following weeks, Aria, Lily, and Mr. Blackwood continued to explore the hidden chambers, cataloging the artifacts and documents they found. They discovered more about the castle's history and the lives of the Blackwood family members who had lived and died within its walls.

One particularly intriguing find was a series of letters between Sir Thomas Blackwood and a mysterious figure known only as "The Alchemist." These letters detailed their collaboration on various experiments and rituals, many of which were aimed at uncovering the secrets of life and death.

"My dear Alchemist,

I have made significant progress in our quest for knowledge. The hidden chamber beneath the castle has yielded many valuable artifacts, and I believe we are close to uncovering the key to eternal life. However, the risks are great, and I must proceed with caution. The spirits grow restless, and I fear that our actions may have unintended consequences."

THE LETTERS PROVIDED a fascinating glimpse into Sir Thomas's mind and his obsession with the occult. They also hinted at the possibility that there were still more hidden chambers and passages within the castle, waiting to be discovered.

Aria felt a renewed sense of purpose as she delved deeper into the castle's history. She was determined to uncover all of its secrets and ensure that the spirits of the Blackwood family could finally find peace.

One evening, as they were exploring the hidden chamber, Aria noticed a loose stone in the wall near the altar. She carefully pried it open, revealing a small, dark passageway. Her heart raced with excitement as she peered inside.

"Look at this," she said, her voice filled with wonder. "There's another passageway behind this wall."

Mr. Blackwood examined the passageway, his expression thoughtful. "This could lead to another hidden chamber. We should investigate."

Aria, Mr. Blackwood, and Lily entered the passageway, their torches casting eerie shadows on the walls. The air was damp and musty, and the narrow corridor seemed to stretch on forever. After several minutes of walking, they reached a heavy wooden door, similar to the one they had found earlier.

Aria pushed the door open, revealing another underground chamber. This one was smaller than the first, but it was filled with even more artifacts and documents. In the center of the room stood a large, ornate chest, its surface covered in intricate carvings and symbols.

"This must be the Alchemist's chamber," Mr. Blackwood said, his voice filled with awe. "These artifacts are incredibly valuable."

Aria approached the chest, her heart pounding with anticipation. She carefully opened it, revealing a collection of ancient books, scrolls, and vials filled with strange liquids.

"These are the Alchemist's writings," she said, her voice trembling with excitement. "They could contain the key to understanding the curse and the rituals Sir Thomas performed."

They spent hours examining the contents of the chest, reading through the Alchemist's notes and experimenting with the various vials and potions. The writings detailed complex alchemical processes and rituals, many of which were aimed at achieving immortality and communicating with the spirit world.

One book, in particular, caught Aria's attention. It was a large, leather-bound volume titled **"The Alchemist's Grimoire."** The book contained detailed instructions for a powerful ritual that could potentially break the curse and free the spirits trapped within the castle.

"This is it," Aria said, her voice filled with excitement. "This grimoire contains the ritual we need."

Mr. Blackwood examined the book, his expression serious. "This ritual is incredibly complex and dangerous. We must proceed with the utmost caution."

Aria nodded, her resolve unwavering. "We've come this far. We can't turn back now."

Over the next few days, they prepared for the ritual, gathering the necessary ingredients and studying the incantations and symbols. They knew that this would be their final attempt to break the curse, and they were determined to succeed.

On the night of the ritual, they gathered in the Alchemist's chamber, their hearts pounding with anticipation. The air was thick with tension, and the flickering torchlight cast eerie shadows on the walls.

Aria stood at the altar, her hands steady as she arranged the ingredients and prepared the incantations. Mr. Blackwood stood beside her, his presence a source of strength and reassurance. Lily watched from the edge of the circle, her eyes filled with concern and hope.

"We are ready," Aria said, her voice steady. "Let's begin."

Mr. Blackwood nodded and began the incantation, his voice resonating through the chamber. Aria joined in, her voice clear and confident. The air grew colder, and the flames of the torches flickered as the ritual took hold.

"Spirits of Blackwood Castle, I summon thee. Come forth and hear my plea."

The crystal ball on the altar began to glow, and a misty figure appeared. It was Lord William, his eyes filled with sorrow and hope.

"Thank you for doing this," he said, his voice echoing through the chamber. "But be warned, the spirits will resist."

As if on cue, the chamber shook, and a dark, malevolent presence filled the air. Aria felt a chill run down her spine as she sensed Edward's spirit entering the room.

"You will not succeed," a voice hissed, filled with venom. "This curse is eternal."

Aria steeled herself, her resolve unwavering. "We will break the curse, Edward. You cannot keep these spirits trapped forever."

The chamber shook violently, and the air grew thick with tension. The torches flickered and went out, plunging the room into darkness. Aria felt a cold hand grasp her arm, and she gasped in fear.

"Hold on!" Mr. Blackwood shouted, his voice barely audible over the commotion. "We must finish the ritual!"

Aria struggled to stay focused, her mind racing. She reached out and grabbed the crystal ball, concentrating all her energy on the spirits of William and Edward.

"Spirits of Blackwood Castle, I command thee. Leave this place and find peace."

The chamber shook again, and the dark presence grew stronger. Aria felt the malevolent energy swirling around her, threatening to overwhelm her. But she remained steadfast, her voice strong and unwavering.

"Leave us in peace, Edward. You cannot keep them here forever."

With a great surge of energy, the dark presence began to dissipate. The room grew still, and the air cleared. Aria felt a sense of relief wash over her as the curse began to lift.

Lord William's figure became more distinct, his expression filled with gratitude. "Thank you, Aria. You have freed us."

Aria felt tears welling up in her eyes. "What will happen now?"

"We will finally find peace," Lord William said, his voice soft and serene. "The curse is broken, and the spirits can move on."

As Lord William's ghost faded away, Aria felt a weight lift from her shoulders. She had done it. They had broken the curse and freed the spirits trapped within the castle.

As dawn broke, Aria, Lily, and Mr. Blackwood sat in the garden, reflecting on the events of the night. The castle seemed lighter, as if a great weight had been lifted. The gardens sparkled in the morning light, and the air was filled with the sound of birdsong.

"You were brave," Mr. Blackwood said, his voice filled with admiration. "Not many would have faced the spirits so fearlessly."

Aria smiled, feeling a sense of accomplishment. "I couldn't have done it without your help. Thank you."

"You have a strong spirit," Mr. Blackwood replied. "The castle is in good hands."

Aria looked out at the sunrise, feeling a sense of peace and belonging. She had inherited more than just a castle; she had inherited a legacy of courage and resilience. And she knew that, whatever challenges lay ahead, she was ready to face them.

Thus began a new chapter in Aria's life, one filled with mystery, adventure, and the promise of new beginnings. She had faced the darkness and emerged stronger, ready to embrace her destiny and the legacy of Blackwood Castle. The future was bright, and she was determined to make the most of it.

Over the following weeks, Aria, Lily, and Mr. Blackwood continued to explore the hidden chambers, cataloging the artifacts and documents they found. They discovered more about the castle's history and the lives of the Blackwood family members who had lived and died within its walls.

One particularly intriguing find was a series of letters between Sir Thomas Blackwood and a mysterious figure known only as "The Alchemist." These letters detailed their collaboration on various experiments and rituals, many of which were aimed at uncovering the secrets of life and death.

"My dear Alchemist,

I have made significant progress in our quest for knowledge. The hidden chamber beneath the castle has yielded many valuable artifacts, and I believe we are close to uncovering the key to eternal life. However, the risks are great, and I must proceed with caution. The spirits grow restless, and I fear that our actions may have unintended consequences."

THE LETTERS PROVIDED a fascinating glimpse into Sir Thomas's mind and his obsession with the occult. They also hinted at the possibility that there were still more hidden chambers and passages within the castle, waiting to be discovered.

Aria felt a renewed sense of purpose as she delved deeper into the castle's history. She was determined to uncover all of its secrets and ensure that the spirits of the Blackwood family could finally find peace.

One evening, as they were exploring the hidden chamber, Aria noticed a loose stone in the wall near the altar. She carefully pried it open, revealing a small, dark passageway. Her heart raced with excitement as she peered inside.

"Look at this," she said, her voice filled with wonder. "There's another passageway behind this wall."

Mr. Blackwood examined the passageway, his expression thoughtful. "This could lead to another hidden chamber. We should investigate."

Aria, Mr. Blackwood, and Lily entered the passageway, their torches casting eerie shadows on the walls. The air was damp and musty, and the narrow corridor seemed to stretch on forever. After several minutes of walking, they reached a heavy wooden door, similar to the one they had found earlier.

Aria pushed the door open, revealing another underground chamber. This one was smaller than the first, but it was filled with even more artifacts and documents. In the center of the room stood a large, ornate chest, its surface covered in intricate carvings and symbols.

"This must be the Alchemist's chamber," Mr. Blackwood said, his voice filled with awe. "These artifacts are incredibly valuable."

Aria approached the chest, her heart pounding with anticipation. She carefully opened it, revealing a collection of ancient books, scrolls, and vials filled with strange liquids.

"These are the Alchemist's writings," she said, her voice trembling with excitement. "They could contain the key to understanding the curse and the rituals Sir Thomas performed."

They spent hours examining the contents of the chest, reading through the Alchemist's notes and experimenting with the various vials and potions. The writings detailed complex alchemical processes and rituals, many of which were aimed at achieving immortality and communicating with the spirit world.

One book, in particular, caught Aria's attention. It was a large, leather-bound volume titled **"The Alchemist's Grimoire."** The book contained detailed instructions for a powerful ritual that could potentially break the curse and free the spirits trapped within the castle.

"This is it," Aria said, her voice filled with excitement. "This grimoire contains the ritual we need."

Mr. Blackwood examined the book, his expression serious. "This ritual is incredibly complex and dangerous. We must proceed with the utmost caution."

Aria nodded, her resolve unwavering. "We've come this far. We can't turn back now."

Over the next few days, they prepared for the ritual, gathering the necessary ingredients and studying the incantations and symbols. They knew that this would be their final attempt to break the curse, and they were determined to succeed.

On the night of the ritual, they gathered in the Alchemist's chamber, their hearts pounding with anticipation. The air was thick with tension, and the flickering torchlight cast eerie shadows on the walls.

Aria stood at the altar, her hands steady as she arranged the ingredients and prepared the incantations. Mr. Blackwood stood beside her, his presence a source of strength and reassurance. Lily watched from the edge of the circle, her eyes filled with concern and hope.

"We are ready," Aria said, her voice steady. "Let's begin."

Mr. Blackwood nodded and began the incantation, his voice resonating through the chamber. Aria joined in, her voice clear and confident. The air grew colder, and the flames of the torches flickered as the ritual took hold.

"Spirits of Blackwood Castle, I summon thee. Come forth and hear my plea."

The crystal ball on the altar began to glow, and a misty figure appeared. It was Lord William, his eyes filled with sorrow and hope.

"Thank you for doing this," he said, his voice echoing through the chamber. "But be warned, the spirits will resist."

As if on cue, the chamber shook, and a dark, malevolent presence filled the air. Aria felt a chill run down her spine as she sensed Edward's spirit entering the room.

"You will not succeed," a voice hissed, filled with venom. "This curse is eternal."

Aria steeled herself, her resolve unwavering. "We will break the curse, Edward. You cannot keep these spirits trapped forever."

The chamber shook violently, and the air grew thick with tension. The torches flickered and went out, plunging the room into darkness. Aria felt a cold hand grasp her arm, and she gasped in fear.

"Hold on!" Mr. Blackwood shouted, his voice barely audible over the commotion. "We must finish the ritual!"

Aria struggled to stay focused, her mind racing. She reached out and grabbed the crystal ball, concentrating all her energy on the spirits of William and Edward.

"Spirits of Blackwood Castle, I command thee. Leave this place and find peace."

The chamber shook again, and the dark presence grew stronger. Aria felt the malevolent energy swirling around her, threatening to overwhelm her. But she remained steadfast, her voice strong and unwavering.

"Leave us in peace, Edward. You cannot keep them here forever."

With a great surge of energy, the dark presence began to dissipate. The room grew still, and the air cleared. Aria felt a sense of relief wash over her as the curse began to lift.

Lord William's figure became more distinct, his expression filled with gratitude. "Thank you, Aria. You have freed us."

Aria felt tears welling up in her eyes. "What will happen now?"

"We will finally find peace," Lord William said, his voice soft and serene. "The curse is broken, and the spirits can move on."

As Lord William's ghost faded away, Aria felt a weight lift from her shoulders. She had done it. They had broken the curse and freed the spirits trapped within the castle.

As dawn broke, Aria, Lily, and Mr. Blackwood sat in the garden, reflecting on the events of the night. The castle seemed lighter, as if a great weight had been lifted. The gardens sparkled in the morning light, and the air was filled with the sound of birdsong.

"You were brave," Mr. Blackwood said, his voice filled with admiration. "Not many would have faced the spirits so fearlessly."

Aria smiled, feeling a sense of accomplishment. "I couldn't have done it without your help. Thank you."

"You have a strong spirit," Mr. Blackwood replied. "The castle is in good hands."

Aria looked out at the sunrise, feeling a sense of peace and belonging. She had inherited more than just a castle; she had inherited a legacy of courage and resilience. And she knew that, whatever challenges lay ahead, she was ready to face them.

Thus began a new chapter in Aria's life, one filled with mystery, adventure, and the promise of new beginnings. She had faced the darkness and emerged stronger, ready to embrace her destiny and the legacy of Blackwood Castle. The future was bright, and she was determined to make the most of it.

Chapter 13: Breaking the Curse

The sense of anticipation was palpable throughout Blackwood Castle as Aria, her friends, and the benevolent spirits prepared for the final ritual to break the curse. The castle itself seemed to hold its breath, waiting for the moment when centuries of torment would finally come to an end. Aria knew that this would be the most challenging endeavor yet, but with the help of her ghostly allies, she felt ready to face whatever came next.

Aria stood in the grand ballroom, surveying the preparations. Candles were placed in a precise circle around the room, their flames flickering gently in the dim light. Mirrors and crystals were strategically positioned to amplify the energy and create a conduit for the spirits. The atmosphere was charged with a mix of fear and hope.

Lily and Mr. Blackwood stood beside her, their expressions a blend of determination and resolve. The benevolent spirits—Lady Eleanor, Annabelle, Thomas, and Margaret—hovered nearby, their presence a source of strength and reassurance.

"We're ready," Aria said, her voice steady. "This is our last chance to break the curse and free the spirits trapped within the castle."

Mr. Blackwood nodded, his eyes filled with admiration. "You have shown great courage and determination, Miss Aria. We are with you."

Lily squeezed Aria's hand, her eyes filled with pride. "We can do this together."

Aria took a deep breath and began the incantation, her voice clear and resonant. "Spirits of Blackwood Castle, I call upon you. Come forth and join us. We seek to bring justice and peace to those who have suffered."

The air grew colder, and a soft breeze seemed to swirl around them. The candle flames flickered, casting eerie patterns on the walls. Aria could feel the presence of the spirits drawing closer, their energy palpable.

"Spirits of Blackwood Castle, I command you to show yourselves."

The crystal ball in the center of the circle began to glow, and a misty figure appeared. It was Lord William, his eyes filled with sorrow and hope.

"Thank you for calling us," Lord William said, his voice echoing softly through the room. "We are here to help you."

Aria nodded, her heart pounding. "Lord William, we have the proof of Edward's betrayal. We know the truth about what happened, and we need your help to break the curse and bring peace to the castle."

Lord William's expression grew determined. "You have done well, Aria. The truth must be revealed, and justice must be served. But be warned, the malevolent spirits will resist. Edward's power is strong, and he will do everything he can to prevent you from succeeding."

Aria steeled herself, her resolve unwavering. "We are ready. Please, help us bring an end to this curse."

The air grew colder still, and Edward's spirit materialized in the circle, his eyes burning with rage. "You dare to summon me?" he hissed, his voice filled with venom. "You cannot break this curse. It is eternal."

Aria held up the letter from William to Eleanor, her voice strong and unwavering. "We have the proof of your betrayal, Edward. This letter reveals your treachery. You poisoned your own brother and used dark magic to bind the spirits of the castle. Your reign of terror ends tonight."

The room shook violently, and the air grew thick with tension. The torches flickered and went out, plunging the room into darkness. Aria felt a cold hand grasp her arm, and she gasped in fear.

"Hold on!" Mr. Blackwood shouted, his voice barely audible over the commotion. "We must stand together!"

Aria struggled to stay focused, her mind racing. She reached out and grabbed the crystal ball, concentrating all her energy on the spirits of William and Edward.

"Spirits of Blackwood Castle, I command thee. Leave this place and find peace. Let the curse be lifted, and justice be done."

The room shook again, and the dark presence grew stronger. Aria felt the malevolent energy swirling around her, threatening to overwhelm her. But she remained steadfast, her voice strong and unwavering.

"Leave us in peace, Edward. You cannot keep them here forever."

With a great surge of energy, the dark presence began to dissipate. The room grew still, and the air cleared. Aria felt a sense of relief wash over her as the curse began to lift.

Edward's spirit screamed in rage, his form becoming more translucent. "This is not over," he hissed. "I will return."

As Edward's spirit faded away, William's form grew more distinct. He looked at Aria with gratitude. "Thank you, Aria. You have freed us."

Aria felt tears welling up in her eyes. "What will happen now?"

"We will finally find peace," William said, his voice soft and serene. "The curse is broken, and the spirits can move on."

As William's ghost faded away, Eleanor's figure became more distinct, her expression filled with gratitude. "Thank you, Aria. You have freed us."

Aria felt a sense of relief wash over her as the curse began to lift. The room grew still, and the air cleared. She had done it. They had broken the curse and freed the spirits trapped within the castle.

As dawn broke, Aria, Lily, and Mr. Blackwood sat in the garden, reflecting on the events of the night. The castle seemed lighter, as if a great weight had been lifted. The gardens sparkled in the morning light, and the air was filled with the sound of birdsong.

"You were brave," Mr. Blackwood said, his voice filled with admiration. "Not many would have faced the spirits so fearlessly."

Aria smiled, feeling a sense of accomplishment. "I couldn't have done it without your help. Thank you."

"You have a strong spirit," Mr. Blackwood replied. "The castle is in good hands."

Aria looked out at the sunrise, feeling a sense of peace and belonging. She had inherited more than just a castle; she had inherited a legacy of courage and resilience. And she knew that, whatever challenges lay ahead, she was ready to face them.

Thus began a new chapter in Aria's life, one filled with mystery, adventure, and the promise of new beginnings. She had faced the darkness and emerged stronger, ready to embrace her destiny and the legacy of Blackwood Castle. The future was bright, and she was determined to make the most of it.

Over the following weeks, Aria, Lily, and Mr. Blackwood continued to explore the hidden chambers, cataloging the artifacts and documents they found. They discovered more about the castle's history and the lives of the Blackwood family members who had lived and died within its walls.

One particularly intriguing find was a series of letters between Sir Thomas Blackwood and a mysterious figure known only as "The Alchemist." These letters detailed their collaboration on various experiments and rituals, many of which were aimed at uncovering the secrets of life and death.

"My dear Alchemist,

I have made significant progress in our quest for knowledge. The hidden chamber beneath the castle has yielded many valuable artifacts, and I believe we are close to uncovering the key to eternal life. However, the risks are great, and I must proceed with caution. The spirits grow restless, and I fear that our actions may have unintended consequences."

THE LETTERS PROVIDED a fascinating glimpse into Sir Thomas's mind and his obsession with the occult. They also hinted at the possibility that there were still more hidden chambers and passages within the castle, waiting to be discovered.

Aria felt a renewed sense of purpose as she delved deeper into the castle's history. She was determined to uncover all of its secrets and ensure that the spirits of the Blackwood family could finally find peace.

One evening, as they were exploring the hidden chamber, Aria noticed a loose stone in the wall near the altar. She carefully pried it open, revealing a small, dark passageway. Her heart raced with excitement as she peered inside.

"Look at this," she said, her voice filled with wonder. "There's another passageway behind this wall."

Mr. Blackwood examined the passageway, his expression thoughtful. "This could lead to another hidden chamber. We should investigate."

Aria, Mr. Blackwood, and Lily entered the passageway, their torches casting eerie shadows on the walls. The air was damp and musty, and the narrow corridor seemed to stretch on forever. After several minutes of walking, they reached a heavy wooden door, similar to the one they had found earlier.

Aria pushed the door open, revealing another underground chamber. This one was smaller than the first, but it was filled with even more artifacts and documents. In the center of the room stood a large, ornate chest, its surface covered in intricate carvings and symbols.

"This must be the Alchemist's chamber," Mr. Blackwood said, his voice filled with awe. "These artifacts are incredibly valuable."

Aria approached the chest, her heart pounding with anticipation. She carefully opened it, revealing a collection of ancient books, scrolls, and vials filled with strange liquids.

"These are the Alchemist's writings," she said, her voice trembling with excitement. "They could contain the key to understanding the curse and the rituals Sir Thomas performed."

They spent hours examining the contents of the chest, reading through the Alchemist's notes and experimenting with the various vials and potions. The writings detailed complex alchemical processes and rituals, many of which were aimed at achieving immortality and communicating with the spirit world.

One book, in particular, caught Aria's attention. It was a large, leather-bound volume titled "**The Alchemist's Grimoire.**" The book contained detailed instructions for a powerful ritual that could potentially break the curse and free the spirits trapped within the castle.

"This is it," Aria said, her voice filled with excitement. "This grimoire contains the ritual we need."

Mr. Blackwood examined the book, his expression serious. "This ritual is incredibly complex and dangerous. We must proceed with the utmost caution."

Aria nodded, her resolve unwavering. "We've come this far. We can't turn back now."

Over the next few days, they prepared for the ritual, gathering the necessary ingredients and studying the incantations and symbols. They knew that this would be their final attempt to break the curse, and they were determined to succeed.

On the night of the ritual, they gathered in the Alchemist's chamber, their hearts pounding with anticipation. The air was thick with tension, and the flickering torchlight cast eerie shadows on the walls.

Aria stood at the altar, her hands steady as she arranged the ingredients and prepared the incantations. Mr. Blackwood stood beside her, his presence a source of strength and reassurance. Lily watched from the edge of the circle, her eyes filled with concern and hope.

"We are ready," Aria said, her voice steady. "Let's begin."

Mr. Blackwood nodded and began the incantation, his voice resonating through the chamber. Aria joined in, her voice clear and confident. The air grew colder, and the flames of the torches flickered as the ritual took hold.

"Spirits of Blackwood Castle, I summon thee. Come forth and hear my plea."

The crystal ball on the altar began to glow, and a misty figure appeared. It was Lord William, his eyes filled with sorrow and hope.

"Thank you for doing this," he said, his voice echoing through the chamber. "But be warned, the spirits will resist."

As if on cue, the chamber shook, and a dark, malevolent presence filled the air. Aria felt a chill run down her spine as she sensed Edward's spirit entering the room.

"You will not succeed," a voice hissed, filled with venom. "This curse is eternal."

Aria steeled herself, her resolve unwavering. "We will break the curse, Edward. You cannot keep these spirits trapped forever."

The chamber shook violently, and the air grew thick with tension. The torches flickered and went out, plunging the room into darkness. Aria felt a cold hand grasp her arm, and she gasped in fear.

"Hold on!" Mr. Blackwood shouted, his voice barely audible over the commotion. "We must finish the ritual!"

Aria struggled to stay focused, her mind racing. She reached out and grabbed the crystal ball, concentrating all her energy on the spirits of William and Edward.

"Spirits of Blackwood Castle, I command thee. Leave this place and find peace."

The chamber shook again, and the dark presence grew stronger. Aria felt the malevolent energy swirling around her, threatening to overwhelm her. But she remained steadfast, her voice strong and unwavering.

"Leave us in peace, Edward. You cannot keep them here forever."

With a great surge of energy, the dark presence began to dissipate. The room grew still, and the air cleared. Aria felt a sense of relief wash over her as the curse began to lift.

Lord William's figure became more distinct, his expression filled with gratitude. "Thank you, Aria. You have freed us."

Aria felt tears welling up in her eyes. "What will happen now?"

"We will finally find peace," Lord William said, his voice soft and serene. "The curse is broken, and the spirits can move on."

As Lord William's ghost faded away, Aria felt a weight lift from her shoulders. She had done it. They had broken the curse and freed the spirits trapped within the castle.

As dawn broke, Aria, Lily, and Mr. Blackwood sat in the garden, reflecting on the events of the night. The castle seemed lighter, as if a great weight had been lifted. The gardens sparkled in the morning light, and the air was filled with the sound of birdsong.

"You were brave," Mr. Blackwood said, his voice filled with admiration. "Not many would have faced the spirits so fearlessly."

Aria smiled, feeling a sense of accomplishment. "I couldn't have done it without your help. Thank you."

"You have a strong spirit," Mr. Blackwood replied. "The castle is in good hands."

Aria looked out at the sunrise, feeling a sense of peace and belonging. She had inherited more than just a castle; she had inherited a legacy of courage and resilience. And she knew that, whatever challenges lay ahead, she was ready to face them.

Thus began a new chapter in Aria's life, one filled with mystery, adventure, and the promise of new beginnings. She had faced the darkness and emerged stronger, ready to embrace her destiny and the legacy of Blackwood Castle. The future was bright, and she was determined to make the most of it.

Chapter 14: A New Beginning

As dawn broke over Blackwood Castle, the first rays of sunlight pierced through the ancient windows, casting a warm, golden hue across the grand hallways and chambers. The castle, once shrouded in darkness and malevolence, now seemed to embrace the light, welcoming a new era of peace and tranquility. Aria stood at one of the tall, arched windows, watching the sunrise with a sense of fulfillment and hope. The curse had been broken, and the spirits that had once haunted the castle were finally at peace.

The transformation of the castle was almost immediate. The oppressive atmosphere that had once hung heavily over every room had lifted, replaced by an air of serenity and calm. The gardens, which had been overgrown and neglected for years, now seemed to bloom with renewed vigor. Birds sang joyfully from the trees, and the scent of fresh flowers filled the air.

Aria took a deep breath, savoring the moment. She knew that her journey was far from over. There was still much work to be done to restore Blackwood Castle to its former glory. But for the first time, she felt truly at home, connected to the history and legacy of the castle in a profound way.

As she stood there, lost in thought, Lily and Mr. Blackwood joined her, their expressions filled with a mixture of relief and determination.

"We did it," Lily said softly, her eyes shining with pride. "The curse is broken."

Mr. Blackwood nodded, his voice filled with admiration. "You showed great courage and strength, Miss Aria. The castle is in good hands."

Aria smiled, feeling a deep sense of gratitude. "Thank you both for your unwavering support. We couldn't have done it without each other. But our work is not yet finished. I want to restore Blackwood Castle to its former glory and turn it into a place of learning and history, a place that honors the spirits that once haunted it."

Lily's eyes lit up with excitement. "That's a wonderful idea, Aria. The castle has so much history and so many stories to tell. It could become a beacon of knowledge and a tribute to the Blackwood family."

Mr. Blackwood's expression grew thoughtful. "Restoring the castle will be a monumental task, but I believe it is a worthy endeavor. The legacy of the Blackwood family deserves to be preserved and honored."

With their resolve strengthened, Aria, Lily, and Mr. Blackwood set about making plans for the restoration of Blackwood Castle. They began by cataloging the artifacts and documents they had discovered during their explorations. The hidden chambers and passageways were filled with treasures that told the story of the Blackwood family's rich and tumultuous history.

One of the first steps in the restoration process was to repair the castle's exterior. The stone walls, weathered by centuries of exposure to the elements, needed to be cleaned and reinforced. Skilled masons were brought in to carefully restore the intricate carvings and sculptures that adorned the castle's facade.

The gardens, once overrun with weeds and neglect, were given new life. Aria and Lily worked tirelessly, planting flowers and shrubs, pruning trees, and creating beautiful pathways that meandered through the lush greenery. The gardens became a sanctuary of peace and beauty, a fitting tribute to the spirits who had once found solace there.

Inside the castle, the grand ballroom, which had been the site of so many significant events, was meticulously restored to its former splendor. The chandeliers sparkled with new brilliance, and the polished floors gleamed in the light. The walls were adorned with portraits and tapestries that depicted the history of the Blackwood family.

Aria also focused on creating spaces for learning and reflection. The library, which had been a treasure trove of knowledge, was expanded and modernized. Comfortable reading nooks were added, and the collection of books was carefully curated to include both historical texts and contemporary works. Aria envisioned the library as a place where scholars and visitors could come to learn about the castle's history and the legacy of the Blackwood family.

As the restoration progressed, word of the castle's transformation began to spread. Visitors from near and far were drawn to Blackwood Castle, eager to explore its rich history and experience its newfound serenity. Aria welcomed them with open arms, sharing the stories of the castle and the spirits who had once inhabited it.

One afternoon, as Aria was giving a tour of the castle to a group of visitors, she found herself in the grand ballroom, standing before the portrait of Lord William and Lady Eleanor. She felt a deep sense of connection to them, as if their spirits were watching over her, guiding her in her efforts to honor their legacy.

"Blackwood Castle is more than just a place," Aria said, addressing the group. "It is a testament to the strength and resilience of the Blackwood family. Their stories, their triumphs and tragedies, have shaped this castle and made it what it is today. We are here to honor their memory and ensure that their legacy lives on."

The visitors listened intently, their expressions filled with awe and reverence. As Aria continued the tour, she felt a sense of fulfillment and purpose. She knew that she was exactly where she was meant to be.

In the months that followed, Aria's vision for Blackwood Castle continued to take shape. She organized events and lectures that brought together historians, scholars, and enthusiasts who were passionate about preserving history and sharing knowledge. The castle became a vibrant hub of activity, a place where people from all walks of life could come together to learn, reflect, and be inspired.

One evening, as Aria was walking through the gardens, she felt a gentle breeze and heard the faint sound of laughter. She knew that the spirits of Blackwood Castle were finally at peace, their souls free from the curse that had bound them for so long. She smiled, feeling a deep sense of contentment and gratitude.

Aria's journey had been filled with challenges and hardships, but she had emerged stronger and more resilient. She had faced the darkness and brought light to a place that had been shrouded in shadows for centuries. And in doing so, she had found her true home and her true purpose.

As she stood in the gardens, watching the sunset, Aria knew that she had found her place within the history of Blackwood Castle. She had become a part of its legacy, a guardian of its stories and a steward of its future. The castle, once a place of fear and sorrow, was now a beacon of hope and inspiration, a testament to the power of love, courage, and resilience.

Thus began a new chapter in Aria's life, one filled with promise and possibility. She had faced the darkness and emerged stronger, ready to embrace her destiny and the legacy of Blackwood Castle. The future was bright, and she was determined to make the most of it.

As the days turned into weeks and the weeks into months, Aria's vision for Blackwood Castle continued to flourish. She organized a series of historical exhibitions that showcased the artifacts and documents they had uncovered, drawing visitors from far and wide. The exhibitions told the story of the Blackwood family's rich and complex history, highlighting their triumphs, struggles, and enduring legacy.

One of the most popular exhibitions was dedicated to the life and legacy of Lord William and Lady Eleanor. The exhibition featured personal letters, portraits, and other artifacts that provided a glimpse into their lives and their enduring love for each other. Visitors were captivated by their story, moved by the depth of their devotion and the tragedy of their untimely deaths.

Aria also worked to establish educational programs that brought schoolchildren and students to the castle. She believed that the next generation should learn about the importance of history and the lessons it could teach. The programs included guided tours, interactive workshops, and lectures by historians and scholars. The children were fascinated by the castle's history, and their enthusiasm brought new energy and vitality to the castle.

As Blackwood Castle continued to thrive, Aria found herself reflecting on her journey and the people who had supported her along the way. She was grateful for the unwavering support of Lily and Mr. Blackwood, who had stood by her side through every challenge and triumph. Their friendship had become a cornerstone of her life, and she knew that she could always count on them.

One evening, as they gathered in the grand ballroom to celebrate the successful completion of another exhibition, Aria raised her glass in a toast. "To Blackwood Castle," she said, her voice filled with emotion. "And to the legacy of the Blackwood family. May their stories continue to inspire and guide us."

Lily and Mr. Blackwood clinked their glasses with hers, their eyes shining with pride and gratitude. "To Blackwood Castle," they echoed, their voices filled with warmth.

As the celebration continued, Aria felt a sense of fulfillment and peace. She had found her true home and her true purpose. Blackwood Castle was more than just a place; it was a living testament to the power of love, courage, and resilience. It was a place where history came alive, where stories were told, and where the past and present intertwined.

In the years that followed, Blackwood Castle continued to grow and evolve. Aria's vision for the castle as a place of learning and history became a reality, attracting visitors from around the world. The castle's exhibitions, events, and educational programs became renowned for their quality and depth, earning accolades and recognition from historians and scholars.

Aria also established a foundation dedicated to the preservation and study of historical sites and artifacts. The foundation provided funding and support for research, conservation, and educational initiatives, ensuring that the legacy of Blackwood Castle would continue for generations to come.

Through it all, Aria remained deeply connected to the spirits of the castle. She often felt their presence, a gentle reminder of the bond they shared. She knew that they were watching over her, guiding her in her efforts to honor their legacy.

One afternoon, as Aria walked through the gardens, she came across a group of children playing near the fountain. They were laughing and running, their faces filled with joy. She smiled, feeling a sense of pride and fulfillment. Blackwood Castle had become a place of life and happiness, a testament to the power of love and resilience.

As she stood there, watching the children, she felt a gentle breeze and heard the faint sound of laughter. She knew that the spirits of Blackwood Castle were finally at peace, their souls free from the curse that had bound them for so long. She smiled, feeling a deep sense of contentment and gratitude.

Aria's journey had been filled with challenges and hardships, but she had emerged stronger and more resilient. She had faced the darkness and brought light to a place that had been shrouded in shadows for centuries. And in doing so, she had found her true home and her true purpose.

As she stood in the gardens, watching the sunset, Aria knew that she had found her place within the history of Blackwood Castle. She had become a part of its legacy, a guardian of its stories and a steward of its future. The castle, once a place of fear and sorrow, was now a beacon of hope and inspiration, a testament to the power of love, courage, and resilience.

Thus began a new chapter in Aria's life, one filled with promise and possibility. She had faced the darkness and emerged stronger, ready to embrace her destiny and the legacy of Blackwood Castle. The future was bright, and she was determined to make the most of it.

Aria's vision for Blackwood Castle continued to evolve, guided by her deep sense of purpose and commitment to honoring the legacy of the Blackwood family. She worked tirelessly to create a space where history and learning were celebrated, where visitors could connect with the past and draw inspiration for the future.

One of the most significant projects she undertook was the restoration of the castle's chapel. The chapel had once been a place of worship and reflection for the Blackwood family, but it had fallen into disrepair over the years. Aria saw the chapel as a symbol of the castle's spiritual heritage and was determined to restore it to its former glory.

With the help of skilled craftsmen and artisans, Aria meticulously restored the chapel's intricate stained glass windows, which depicted scenes from the Bible and the history of the Blackwood family. The wooden pews were repaired and polished, and the altar was restored to its original beauty. The chapel became a place of quiet contemplation and reverence, a sanctuary for visitors seeking solace and inspiration.

As part of the restoration, Aria also commissioned a memorial to honor the spirits who had once haunted the castle. The memorial, located in the chapel's garden, featured a beautiful sculpture of Lord William and Lady Eleanor, their hands intertwined in a gesture of eternal love and unity. The inscription on the memorial read:

"In memory of the Blackwood family, whose courage, love, and resilience shall forever inspire us. May their spirits find peace and their legacy endure."

THE MEMORIAL BECAME a focal point for visitors, a place where they could pay their respects and reflect on the powerful stories of the Blackwood family. It also served as a reminder of the castle's transformation from a place of darkness to one of light and hope.

As Aria stood before the memorial, she felt a deep sense of fulfillment and gratitude. She knew that she had honored the legacy of the Blackwood family in a meaningful way, ensuring that their stories would be remembered and celebrated for generations to come.

One evening, as the sun set over the castle, Aria gathered with Lily and Mr. Blackwood in the grand ballroom. The room, once filled with shadows and fear, now radiated warmth and beauty. They stood together, looking out over the gardens as the last rays of sunlight bathed the castle in a golden glow.

"We've come a long way," Aria said, her voice filled with emotion. "Blackwood Castle has become a place of light and hope, a testament to the power of love and resilience."

Lily smiled, her eyes shining with pride. "You've created something truly special, Aria. The castle's legacy will continue to inspire and guide us."

Mr. Blackwood nodded, his expression filled with admiration. "You have honored the Blackwood family in the most profound way. The castle is in good hands, and its future is bright."

As they stood together, watching the sunset, Aria felt a sense of peace and belonging. She had found her true home and her true purpose. Blackwood Castle was more than just a place; it was a living testament to the power of love, courage, and resilience. It was a place where history came alive, where stories were told, and where the past and present intertwined.

Thus began a new chapter in Aria's life, one filled with promise and possibility. She had faced the darkness and emerged stronger, ready to embrace her destiny and the legacy of Blackwood Castle. The future was bright, and she was determined to make the most of it.

As the days turned into weeks and the weeks into months, Aria's vision for Blackwood Castle continued to flourish. She organized a series of historical exhibitions that showcased the artifacts and documents they had uncovered, drawing visitors from far and wide. The exhibitions told the story of the Blackwood family's rich and complex history, highlighting their triumphs, struggles, and enduring legacy.

One of the most popular exhibitions was dedicated to the life and legacy of Lord William and Lady Eleanor. The exhibition featured personal letters, portraits, and other artifacts that provided a glimpse into their lives and their enduring love for each other. Visitors were captivated by their story, moved by the depth of their devotion and the tragedy of their untimely deaths.

Aria also worked to establish educational programs that brought schoolchildren and students to the castle. She believed that the next generation should learn about the importance of history and the lessons it could teach. The programs included guided tours, interactive workshops, and lectures by historians and scholars. The children were fascinated by the castle's history, and their enthusiasm brought new energy and vitality to the castle.

As Blackwood Castle continued to thrive, Aria found herself reflecting on her journey and the people who had supported her along the way. She was grateful for the unwavering support of Lily and Mr. Blackwood, who had stood by her side through every challenge and triumph. Their friendship had become a cornerstone of her life, and she knew that she could always count on them.

One evening, as they gathered in the grand ballroom to celebrate the successful completion of another exhibition, Aria raised her glass in a toast. "To Blackwood Castle," she said, her voice filled with emotion. "And to the legacy of the Blackwood family. May their stories continue to inspire and guide us."

Lily and Mr. Blackwood clinked their glasses with hers, their eyes shining with pride and gratitude. "To Blackwood Castle," they echoed, their voices filled with warmth.

As the celebration continued, Aria felt a sense of fulfillment and peace. She had found her true home and her true purpose. Blackwood Castle was more than just a place; it was a living testament to the power of love, courage, and resilience. It was a place where history came alive, where stories were told, and where the past and present intertwined.

In the years that followed, Blackwood Castle continued to grow and evolve. Aria's vision for the castle as a place of learning and history became a reality, attracting visitors from around the world. The castle's exhibitions, events, and educational programs became renowned for their quality and depth, earning accolades and recognition from historians and scholars.

Aria also established a foundation dedicated to the preservation and study of historical sites and artifacts. The foundation provided funding and support for research, conservation, and educational initiatives, ensuring that the legacy of Blackwood Castle would continue for generations to come.

Through it all, Aria remained deeply connected to the spirits of the castle. She often felt their presence, a gentle reminder of the bond they shared. She knew that they were watching over her, guiding her in her efforts to honor their legacy.

One afternoon, as Aria walked through the gardens, she came across a group of children playing near the fountain. They were laughing and running, their faces filled with joy. She smiled, feeling a sense of pride and fulfillment. Blackwood Castle had become a place of life and happiness, a testament to the power of love and resilience.

As she stood there, watching the children, she felt a gentle breeze and heard the faint sound of laughter. She knew that the spirits of Blackwood Castle were finally at peace, their souls free from the curse that had bound them for so long. She smiled, feeling a deep sense of contentment and gratitude.

Aria's journey had been filled with challenges and hardships, but she had emerged stronger and more resilient. She had faced the darkness and brought light to a place that had been shrouded in shadows for centuries. And in doing so, she had found her true home and her true purpose.

As she stood in the gardens, watching the sunset, Aria knew that she had found her place within the history of Blackwood Castle. She had become a part of its legacy, a guardian of its stories and a steward of its future. The castle, once a place of fear and sorrow, was now a beacon of hope and inspiration, a testament to the power of love, courage, and resilience.

Thus began a new chapter in Aria's life, one filled with promise and possibility. She had faced the darkness and emerged stronger, ready to embrace her destiny and the legacy of Blackwood Castle. The future was bright, and she was determined to make the most of it.

Chapter 15: The Legacy

Years had passed since Aria first arrived at Blackwood Castle, drawn by the mysterious invitation that had set her on a path of discovery and transformation. The castle, once a place of darkness and fear, had been reborn as a beacon of history, learning, and inspiration. Its storied halls and chambers, now meticulously restored, attracted visitors from around the world, eager to learn about the rich legacy of the Blackwood family.

Aria stood in the grand ballroom, the very room where she had faced the malevolent spirits and broken the centuries-old curse. The chandeliers sparkled overhead, casting a warm glow across the polished floors and intricately decorated walls. The air was filled with the hum of conversation and the occasional burst of laughter, as guests mingled and admired the historical exhibits on display.

As a respected historian and the curator of Blackwood Castle, Aria had dedicated her life to preserving its history and sharing its stories. She had written numerous books and articles about the Blackwood family, their triumphs and tragedies, and the events that had shaped the castle's legacy. Her work had earned her recognition and accolades, but more importantly, it had ensured that the spirits of the castle would never be forgotten.

Aria walked through the ballroom, her heart filled with a sense of fulfillment and pride. She greeted guests and answered their questions, sharing anecdotes and insights about the castle's history. As she spoke, she couldn't help but reflect on her own journey and the friends she had made along the way.

Lily, her loyal and steadfast companion, was now a renowned garden designer. Her work in restoring the castle's gardens had earned her international acclaim, and she continued to collaborate with Aria on various projects.

Together, they had transformed the castle's grounds into a paradise of beauty and tranquility, a fitting tribute to the spirits who had once found solace there.

Mr. Blackwood, the last living descendant of the Blackwood family, had become a close and trusted friend. His knowledge and wisdom had been invaluable in their efforts to uncover the castle's secrets and restore its legacy. Despite the revelation of his family's dark past, he had dedicated himself to making amends and ensuring that the history of Blackwood Castle was preserved with honesty and integrity.

As Aria mingled with the guests, she spotted Mr. Blackwood standing near one of the exhibits, deep in conversation with a group of historians. She made her way over to him, smiling as he looked up and greeted her with a nod.

"Miss Aria," he said, his voice filled with warmth. "You have outdone yourself once again. The exhibits are truly magnificent."

Aria blushed, feeling a surge of pride. "Thank you, Mr. Blackwood. It has been a labor of love, and I couldn't have done it without your support."

One of the historians, a distinguished-looking man with silver hair, turned to Aria with a curious expression. "I must say, Miss Aria, your work on the Blackwood family history is nothing short of extraordinary. How did you manage to uncover so much about their lives and their legacy?"

Aria smiled, her thoughts drifting back to the many long nights spent poring over ancient documents and exploring hidden chambers. "It was a combination of perseverance, curiosity, and the guidance of some very special friends."

The historian raised an eyebrow. "Friends, you say? I imagine the spirits of Blackwood Castle must have had quite a story to tell."

Aria's smile widened. "Indeed they did. Their stories are woven into the very fabric of this castle, and it has been my honor to share them with the world."

As the evening progressed, Aria found herself drawn to the chapel garden, where the memorial to Lord William and Lady Eleanor stood. The garden was bathed in the soft light of the setting sun, and the air was filled with the scent of blooming flowers. She walked over to the memorial, feeling a deep sense of connection to the spirits who had guided her on her journey.

She stood before the sculpture of Lord William and Lady Eleanor, their hands intertwined in a gesture of eternal love and unity. The inscription on the memorial read:

"In memory of the Blackwood family, whose courage, love, and resilience shall forever inspire us. May their spirits find peace and their legacy endure."

ARIA FELT A TEAR SLIP down her cheek as she read the words, her heart filled with gratitude. The Blackwood family had faced unimaginable challenges and hardships, but their love and resilience had endured. Their legacy had become a source of inspiration and hope, a testament to the power of the human spirit.

As she stood there, lost in thought, she felt a gentle breeze and heard the faint sound of laughter. She knew that the spirits of Blackwood Castle were watching over her, their presence a comforting reminder of the bond they shared.

"Thank you," she whispered, her voice filled with emotion. "Thank you for guiding me and for allowing me to be a part of your story. I will honor your legacy for as long as I live."

As the sun dipped below the horizon, casting a warm, golden glow across the garden, Aria felt a sense of closure. Her journey had been filled with challenges and hardships, but it had also been a journey of discovery, growth, and transformation. She had found her true home and her true purpose, and she knew that the legacy of Blackwood Castle would continue to inspire future generations.

With a renewed sense of determination, Aria turned and made her way back to the grand ballroom, where the celebration continued. She was greeted by the smiling faces of her friends and colleagues, their eyes filled with admiration and respect.

"To Blackwood Castle," she said, raising her glass in a toast. "And to the legacy of the Blackwood family. May their stories continue to inspire and guide us."

As the guests echoed her toast, Aria felt a sense of peace and fulfillment. The castle, once a place of darkness and fear, had become a beacon of light and hope. Its history and legacy had been preserved and honored, and its future was filled with promise and possibility.

In the years that followed, Blackwood Castle continued to thrive as a renowned historical site. Visitors from around the world came to explore its rich history and to be inspired by the stories of the Blackwood family. Aria, now a respected historian and curator, continued to share the castle's legacy with passion and dedication.

Her work at Blackwood Castle earned her numerous accolades and recognition, but more importantly, it allowed her to fulfill her true purpose. She had become a guardian of history, a steward of the past, and a beacon of inspiration for the future.

One evening, as Aria sat in her study, surrounded by books and documents, she reflected on her journey and the friends she had made, both living and dead. She thought of Lord William and Lady Eleanor, whose love and resilience had become a source of inspiration for her. She thought of Annabelle, Thomas, and Margaret, whose courage and sacrifice had guided her in her quest to break the curse. And she thought of Lily and Mr. Blackwood, whose unwavering support and friendship had been her anchor through it all.

As she wrote in her journal, documenting the latest discoveries and insights about the Blackwood family, she felt a sense of closure and fulfillment. Her journey at Blackwood Castle had been an adventure filled with challenges, but it had also been a journey of growth, discovery, and transformation.

Aria closed her journal and looked out the window, watching as the stars began to twinkle in the night sky. She knew that her work was far from over. There were still stories to uncover, histories to preserve, and legacies to honor. And she was ready to embrace whatever new adventures lay ahead.

As she sat there, lost in thought, she heard a gentle knock on the door. It was Lily, her eyes filled with excitement.

"Aria, there's someone here to see you," she said, her voice filled with anticipation.

Aria stood up, curiosity piqued. She followed Lily to the grand ballroom, where a young woman stood, holding a letter in her hand. The woman looked nervous but determined, her eyes filled with a mixture of hope and fear.

"Miss Aria," the woman said, her voice trembling slightly. "My name is Emily, and I have a story to tell you. It's about my family and an old, mysterious castle we inherited. I think you might be able to help us."

Aria's heart quickened with anticipation. She had always believed that her work at Blackwood Castle was just the beginning, that there were other stories waiting to be uncovered, other legacies to be preserved.

"Emily, I'd be honored to hear your story," Aria said, her voice filled with warmth and sincerity. "Let's sit down and talk."

As they sat together in the grand ballroom, the same room where Aria had once faced the malevolent spirits and broken the curse, she felt a sense of excitement and possibility. Her journey at Blackwood Castle had prepared her for whatever new adventures lay ahead, and she was ready to embrace them with open arms.

The legacy of Blackwood Castle had become a part of her, a testament to the power of love, courage, and resilience. And as she listened to Emily's story, she knew that her work as a historian and guardian of history was far from over.

The future was filled with promise and possibility, and Aria was determined to make the most of it. The legacy of Blackwood Castle would continue to inspire and guide her, as she embarked on new adventures and uncovered new stories, ensuring that the past would always be remembered and honored.

As the night wore on, and the stars twinkled in the sky, Aria felt a deep sense of fulfillment and peace. Her journey had come full circle, and she was ready for whatever new challenges and adventures lay ahead. The legacy of Blackwood Castle would live on, a beacon of light and hope for generations to come.

And so, with a heart full of gratitude and a spirit ready for new adventures, Aria embraced the future, knowing that the stories of the past would always guide her, and the legacy of Blackwood Castle would forever inspire her.

The End

Don't miss out!

Visit the website below and you can sign up to receive emails whenever Sarah Elizabeth Davis publishes a new book. There's no charge and no obligation.

https://books2read.com/r/B-A-METXB-NQGDE

BOOKS 2 READ

Connecting independent readers to independent writers.

Did you love *The Haunted Castle*? Then you should read *The Sorcerer's Spellbook*[1] by Sarah Elizabeth Davis!

[2]

Step into a world where magic and mystery intertwine in *The Sorcerer's Spellbook: An Anthology*. This collection of enchanting tales begins with the prologue, introducing the legendary Spellbook, a tome of immense power. From the creation of the Spellbook to its far-reaching impact, each chapter reveals captivating stories: a cursed village, elemental guardians, time manipulation, and more. Follow diverse characters as they navigate the Spellbook's spells, facing challenges, ethical dilemmas, and the transformative power of magic. The epilogue ties together these adventures, highlighting the Spellbook's enduring legacy and the boundless potential of its magic.

---

1. https://books2read.com/u/49515p

2. https://books2read.com/u/49515p

About the Author

Sarah Elizabeth Davis is a celebrated author in the fantasy collections and anthologies genre. Known for her captivating storytelling, she crafts intricate tales that transport readers to magical realms. Raised in a town rich with folklore, her passion for fantasy was kindled early on. With a degree in English Literature, Sarah has published acclaimed anthologies, earning a loyal following. When not writing, she enjoys exploring new places and spending time with family and pets. Sarah's work, filled with wonder and adventure, continues to enchant readers and leave a lasting impact on the literary world.